D0815959

Dear Romance Reader,

Welcome to a world of breathtaking passion and never-ending romance.
Welcome to *Precious Gem Romances*.

It is our pleasure to present *Precious Gem Romances*, a wonderful new line of romance books by some of America's best-loved authors. Let these thrilling historical and contemporary romances sweep you away to far-off times and places in stories that will dazzle your senses and melt your heart.

Sparkling with joy, laughter, and love, each *Precious Gem Romance* glows with all the passion and excitement you expect from the very best in romance. Offered at a great affordable price, these books are an irresistible value—and an essential addition to your romance collection. Tender love stories you will want to read again and again, *Precious Gem Romances* are books you will treasure forever.

Look for fabulous new *Precious Gem Romances* each month—available only at Wal★Mart.

Kate Duffy
Editorial Director

COURTING
MANDY

VICTORIA
CHANCELLOR

Zebra Books
Kensington Publishing Corp.

http://www.zebrabooks.com

ZEBRA BOOKS are published by

Kensington Publishing Corp.
850 Third Avenue
New York, NY 10022

Zebra and the Z logo Reg. U.S. Pat. & TM Off.

First Printing: April, 1999
10   9   8   7   6   5   4   3   2   1

Printed in the United States of America

To my brother-in-law, John C. Garrett—
a "bad boy" who rode into my
sister's life many years ago—
with fond memories.
Thanks for the lessons on life.

CHAPTER ONE

Mandy Thompson balanced a stack of books on her hip while reaching for the phone. She hadn't hooked up an answering machine at the temporary library yet, and whoever was trying to reach her was letting the number ring, and ring, and ring.

"Hello," she answered breathlessly, setting the children's books down on an unopened box of paperback donations.

"Mandy, dear, I'm so glad we reached you," Millicent Gardner said in her sing-song, sweeter-than-pie voice. "Greta told me to call when he first left, but I got another phone call from—"

"Before who left, Millicent?"

"Oh, our nephew. He's on his way over to see you, riding that new bike of his. You remember the pledge we made to the library building fund? Well, he's coming by with the check."

"Oh, that's great, Millicent. Thank you, and please

thank Greta for me also.'' Mandy craned her neck to look out the front windows of the former bookstore. She didn't see any children approaching, but the boy would probably be here any minute. Greta and Millicent didn't live too far away.

"We're really pleased that you've taken on this project, Mandy. Scottsville needs a new library, but that awful fire was a bad way to get one.''

"Yes, I know.'' As Mandy searched for the Gardner sisters' nephew, she saw something quite out of place in Scottsville, something quite unusual for any small East Texas town, and quite . . . interesting.

"I'll talk to you later, Mandy. Greta is looking for the remote control, and you know how grouchy she can be when she can't find something.''

Mandy knew no such thing, but absently agreed as she said goodbye and hung up the phone. Or at least she thought she'd said goodbye. Her attention was so riveted on the man outside the window that she wasn't real sure.

Dressed in a black leather jacket, his hair windblown, his angular face shadowed by at least a few day's stubble of beard, he looked like something from a Harley-Davidson poster. Falling yellow and orange leaves swirled around him as sunlight filtered through the pine trees and gilded him in gold. He straddled a massive motorcycle the way a knight of old sat his trusty war horse. Even more than thirty feet away, through a closed door and a plate glass window, Mandy felt the vibrations of the powerful machine as it idled in the autumn afternoon.

Why was he stopped there so long? Granted, the intersection boasted one of Scottsville's few four-way stops, but there was little traffic this late in the afternoon on Sunday. Most people were either getting ready for evening church services or eating dinner with their families.

He ran a hand through his dark, already tousled hair. Mandy's pulse rose a few beats as she watched him take a deep breath. His white T-shirt molded to a broad chest and a flat, muscular abdomen. She swallowed a lump in her throat as her gaze roamed down his long, jeans-clad legs to the black boots that were braced arrogantly on the pavement.

Definitely advertising material. Mandy tore her gaze from the man for just a moment to make sure a camera and crew weren't filming the very sexy man on the gleaming motorcycle.

Nope. Not another soul around. He must be lost. Maybe he needed directions. Maybe she should stick her head out the door and ask if he needed help. After all, that would be the neighborly thing to do.

As if a small-town librarian was the type of "neighbor" this dangerous-looking stranger would find interesting.

With a sigh, Mandy realized she'd allowed herself to get distracted again. Darn it. She'd come to Scottsville to avoid this sort of thing. She couldn't allow herself to give in to a merely physical attraction.

She turned away from the window and retrieved the stack of books, hoping the stranger found his way out of town before she was tempted to walk outside, throw her leg over the big chrome machine, and ride out of town with him.

Besides, she had to get these books sorted into early readers and picture books. Some of the people who had packed the salvaged books after the fire in the old library hadn't been too particular about which books they'd thrown into which boxes.

And the Gardner sisters' nephew was on his way over with a donation for the new library. Watching the town's upstanding librarian riding off on the back of a motorcycle would not be a good sight for a young boy to see.

Perhaps the boy would like to borrow a few of the books while he was in town visiting his aunts. Mandy didn't know the Gardner sisters real well, but who could be unaware of two of the town's most recognized citizens? She'd realized early on that the elderly women cared deeply about this town. They also baked absolutely wonderful cookies, muffins, and rolls in their bakery on the square.

This nephew must be their great nephew. Surely they didn't have siblings young enough to have a child. Unless, of course, a brother had married a much younger woman. That would explain . . .

A blast of crisp autumn wind blew through the temporary library as the door opened, startling Mandy out of her contemplation. She turned, a smile on her face as she anticipated meeting the Gardner nephew.

But the man standing in front of her didn't resemble a child in the least. All black leather, tight jeans, and lean, muscular male, he was far too intriguing for her peace of mind, far too tempting for any mortal woman. He *definitely* wasn't from around here. Her eyes widened as a slow smile creased his lean, stubbled cheeks.

"Hi," he said in a deep, sexy voice that vibrated through her like the throbbing of his motorcycle. "You must be the new librarian."

"Yes," she managed to say, blinking her eyes when

she realized she'd been staring. "Yes, but how did you know . . . ?"

He reached inside his black leather jacket and pulled out an envelope. "There aren't too many secrets in a small town." He grinned, probably at the confused look on her face. "I'm Case Gardner, Greta and Millicent's nephew. Sure am glad to meet you, Miss Mandy Thompson."

Case had figured his aunts had an ulterior motive when they insisted he take their Scottsville Public Library building fund donation to the new librarian before he'd even finished unpacking. He just hadn't figured on his own interest in the new librarian Greta and Millicent had raved about.

Mandy Thompson was pretty, but she went out of her way to downplay her big brown eyes, shiny hair, and slim figure. Dressed in rather baggy chinos and a rust-colored sweater, she appeared awfully young to be hidden away in a library. Her brown hair held a hint of red highlights. Since she'd secured it in a low ponytail, he couldn't tell how the strands would feel when he ran his fingers through them. But her skin . . . she had a creamy, ivory complexion he longed to touch.

"You're the nephew?" she asked, her eyes round with surprise, her right arm holding several oversized children's books in front of her like a shield.

"The one and only," he replied, hoping she wasn't going to be this nervous or confused around him for the rest of his stay in town. He loved libraries, especially small, cozy ones run by single, attractive librarians.

"I was expecting someone a little . . . younger," she said as she held out her hand for the envelope he offered.

Case chuckled and shook his head. "My aunts can be a little vague on details." He passed the donation to her, wishing he could get a little closer without frightening her. He supposed he did look disreputable with his black leather jacket, motorcycle boots, and three day's growth of beard.

"I just got into town this afternoon, but they insisted I come by right away. They said something about forgetting to bring the donation to the last meeting of the Friends of the Library."

"Yes . . . well, I'm glad you came by." Mandy shifted the books closer to her chest, tilting her chin up ever so slightly. At the moment, she looked more like a prissy schoolmarm than a modern librarian.

"Need any help?" he asked, hooking his hands in his back pockets so he wouldn't be tempted to reach out and pry those picture books out of her white-knuckled grip.

"No!" She said the word so quickly, so emphatically, that a less persistent man might be tempted to walk out and dismiss any hopes of courting Miss Mandy Thompson. But she gave off a lot of clues as to what she was really feeling that he couldn't ignore, and Case couldn't resist a good mystery.

He was just about to offer again when he noticed her gaze drifting southward, roaming over him with the sensation of a dozen soft feathers. Her eyes round and nearly transfixed, she seemed to be memorizing him with her eyes. As a matter of fact, he felt darn near consumed by her hot look, the feeling causing an entirely predictable reaction, which he tried to hide by shifting his weight and unhooking his hands from his back pockets.

She turned guilty eyes upward, meeting his gaze with a startled one of her own. A delicate peach blush lit up that ivory skin, making Case think of rosy dawns and rumpled sheets.

"On second thought, I'd better get back to the house. Greta might need some help."

Mandy nodded, swallowing hard. "It was nice meeting you, Mr. Gardner," she managed to say, although her voice sounded a bit husky.

"My pleasure," he said with a slow smile he couldn't hold back even if he'd wanted to—which he didn't. He hoped to cause her just a fraction of the discomfort she had inflicted on him with those ravishing eyes of hers.

She threw her other arm around the books and hugged them to the center of her chest. Case was certain her breasts were squished flat against her ribs.

"Please thank your aunts for me. We can use all the donations we can get."

"Really? Well, I'll just see what I can do to help."

She opened her mouth to speak. Case had the feeling she was about to say "no" again, but then thought better of being so hasty or rude. Not that he'd take offense. He found her reaction to him just one more tantalizing clue to the mystery of Mandy Thompson, small town librarian.

She offered a weak smile as she backed up, almost tripping over a box. Case took that as his clue to leave. No sense in making her fall all over herself. She already seemed nervous enough around him.

"Have a nice visit in Scottsville."

"Oh, I'm sure I'll be seeing you again. You see,

I'm going to be here for a while. With Greta's broken ankle and Millicent's—well, let's just call it her lack of business sense—I've got my work cut out for me."

"Work?"

"Yes. This isn't just a weekend stay. You see, I'm going to be helping out in the bakery until Greta is up and around again." Case grinned at Mandy's dumbstruck expression. "Since both my aunts told me you're a regular customer, I'm sure I'll see you often."

"You're going to *bake*?"

"Now don't be so skeptical. I think I can manage to stir up some flour and sugar and whatever else. And I know how to make change and smile at the customers. What else do I need to know?" he asked.

"I'm not sure. I've never worked in a bakery."

"Neither have I, but there's a first time for everything."

"And a last time."

Case shrugged. "Maybe I'll be a really great baker. I might have a new career."

Mandy looked even more dubious about that idea. "Then I wish you luck, Mr. Gardner, because I'm sure there's more to running the bakery than you might imagine."

"Please, call me Case."

She nodded, clutching the books even tighter. He noticed she didn't invite him to call her Mandy, but then, he didn't feel he needed an invitation.

"I'm an optimist," he explained in answer to her earlier comment about the rigors of running a bakery. "I'm looking at this as an adventure."

Mandy shuddered, but her eyes seemed bright with excitement. "You probably have lots of those."

"As many as I can. Haven't you heard? Life is short."

"So are some people's memories."

Case chuckled and shook his head. "I can tell you're a cynic. I think maybe you've been working too hard."

"Yes, and speaking of that . . ."

"Okay, I can take a hint," he said with a smile. If he'd been wearing a cowboy hat, he would have tipped it as he headed for the door. But today, he was a biker, even if he was in Texas. "Good afternoon, Mandy Thompson," he said, unable to keep the humor out of his voice as he took one last look at her confounded expression.

She didn't look like a cynic when she devoured him with her big, expressive brown eyes. It was more as if she was optimistic about getting to know him better even as she told herself she shouldn't.

He walked down the three steps to the cracked concrete sidewalk leading from the street to the temporary library. The crisp autumn air felt good against his heated skin. If he looked in a mirror, he'd bet he appeared as flushed as the woman inside.

Of course, he thought, running a hand over his scratchy cheeks, she probably hadn't noticed since he was a bit grubby to begin with. First thing on his agenda after he finished unpacking was a long, hot shower and a shave. Case might not live a totally conventional life, but that didn't mean he had to look like a bum. He had a feeling that once he looked a bit more presentable, he'd make a lot more headway with the town librarian.

Smiling into the lengthening shadows of afternoon, he dug his keys out of his front pocket and swung his leg over his new Harley. He turned the key, and the bike roared to life with a pulsing rhythm Case found intoxicating. He'd have to get Mandy on this monster machine, he thought as he kicked off the stand and pulled away from the curb. She'd probably crush him to her in the same way she'd held those books. He could almost feel her breasts pressed tightly against his back.

Shifting in the seat, he revised his earlier plan. Perhaps a short, hot shower to get the road dirt off, followed by a long, cold one to get his mind off the woman who was intriguing enough to be the heroine of a Casey Flannigan novel.

He would be working in the bakery. Mandy let out a sigh of frustration as she sank onto her bed later that night.

She reached over and turned off the light, settling back against the cool cotton-blend sheets and fluffy polyester-filled pillows, pulling the blanket up to her chin. Sensible, no-nonsense bed linens, just like the flannel nightshirt and white socks she wore to bed, the orthopedically sound walking shoes she used every day, and the practical clothes that she donned for work during the week. Her whole life was centered around propriety, schedules, and meaningful work.

It was not the most exciting life, but that was just the point. If she'd wanted fun and games, challenges and diversions, she would have stayed in Dallas. There had been plenty of complications there.

Except, she'd never seen anything as tempting as Case Gardner, even at the hottest singles bar or the best fitness centers.

Punching her pillow and frowning into the darkness, Mandy rolled to her side. She didn't need the distraction of seeing Greta and Millicent's nephew every morning, but she wasn't about to change her schedule to avoid the bakery. She'd just learn to adjust, that was all.

The next time she saw him, she'd have herself under control. She'd be wearing the "uniform" of a small town librarian. She'd remind herself that gorgeous men with great big motorcycles should be avoided. She'd tell herself that she loved her life: the quiet, small house she'd rented, the library that needed rebuilding, the good friends she'd made.

Then and only then would she be immune to his disreputable good looks and charismatic grin.

But as she drifted off to sleep, she couldn't help but wonder what other kinds of jobs Case had held, and if he even had a career he'd put on hold to become a baker in a small East Texas town.

CHAPTER TWO

"And then you just sprinkle the nuts over the dough and roll it up," Millicent said, moving through the process of creating cinnamon rolls with a speed that belied her advanced years. Case chided himself silently for ever thinking that his aunt was a bit feeble. He couldn't keep up with her instructions any more than he could take apart the engine of his motorcycle and put it back together again.

Of course, the extremely early hour and lack of coffee might have something to do with his inability to concentrate. He had never considered himself a morning person.

Rubbing one hand over his scratchy eyes, he gently placed the other hand over Millicent's busy but arthritic fingers. "Just a minute, Aunt Millie. Cinnamon rolls are a little advanced for me. I think maybe I'd better concentrate on making the coffee."

* * *

By the time they opened at seven o'clock, Millicent was raring to go but Case was ready to call it a day. However, he knew enough to smile as the first customers came in. A man who commuted to Tyler stopped for a breakfast of muffins, milk, and coffee; a mother and daughter who'd gotten up early came in for a treat before school; two schoolteachers visited every morning. Millicent introduced him to everyone, but he doubted he'd remember their names tomorrow morning. Maybe he should start making a list.

By eight-thirty, he'd taken off his denim shirt and lost count of the number of cookies he'd put into and taken out of the oven. His aunt continued to introduce him to everyone, but now he simply looked over his shoulder, smiled, and said hello. He didn't figure anyone wanted to shake hands, since he was covered in blobs of dough, several colors of those sprinkly things his aunts put on the butter cookies, and an overall light dusting of flour.

He would probably frighten small children, but fortunately, they'd quit coming in some time ago as this was a school day.

"Oh, Case, you met our new librarian yesterday, didn't you?" Millicent called out in her melodious voice.

Case grimaced as he stood facing the hot ovens. He couldn't look worse. Yesterday, he'd been grubby from his three-day trip to Scottsville. Today, he looked like a true doughboy. Still, he couldn't ignore Miss Mandy Thompson—not if he was going to pursue the attraction he knew was mutual.

Or maybe not after she saw how ridiculous he must look today.

Taking a deep breath, he smiled and turned around. "Hello, Mandy."

Her eyes widened, much as they had yesterday, but didn't register nearly as much admiration as before. Instead, her look of surprise quickly turned to amusement.

"Hello . . . Case," she said, obviously trying to keep from laughing.

She looked anything but laughable with her shiny reddish-brown hair brushing against the perfect ivory skin of her jawline. However, she obviously hadn't dressed to catch a man's attention. Her shapeless dark blue dress with the little yellow flowers would have looked perfect on another woman—like maybe his seventy-eight-year-old aunt.

"Oh, my," Millicent said, as if seeing him for the first time. "Case has been working so hard to learn this business. I'm afraid I might have given him a little too much for his first day."

"I'm fine, Aunt Millie. I just look like h . . . heck."

"No, no," Millicent said, fluttering her hands. "You need to take a little break. Have one of these muffins you baked, and I'll pour you another cup of coffee."

He glanced from his aunt to Mandy. Apparently, she'd just realized that dear Millicent was doing her level best to get them together. A peachy blush stained her cheeks, and she looked as though she couldn't decide whether to run out the door or burst out laughing.

Millicent took the decision away from her, bustling over with two cups of coffee before either he or Mandy could take their eyes off each other. "Now you two just sit down and have a nice cup of coffee and one of those fresh blueberry muffins. Case made these himself, Mandy."

"A man who can cook," she muttered under her breath.

"Bake," he corrected. "I'm not much of a cook."

"Well, of course you're not, dear. You're a—"

"I'm a mess," Case said quickly, cutting off his aunt's comments. "While I'm in Scottsville, I'm just working in the bakery, remember?" He hoped Millicent took the hint that he didn't want to discuss his personal life . . . at least, not yet. "I think I'd better clean up a little first. I feel like I'm already wearing my breakfast."

Mandy sat perfectly straight in the chrome and vinyl chair, resisting the urge to fidget with her hair or clasp her hands nervously in her lap. Instead, she rested her wrists on the Formica tabletop and waited for Case to emerge from the restroom.

She'd been surprised to see him this morning, a bit tired and sweaty, his back to her as he tended the hot oven. Dressed in a body-hugging white T-shirt and tight, faded jeans, his shoulders looked even wider, his waist trimmer, and his . . .

"Don't go there," she muttered to herself, so flustered that she stirred her already sweetened coffee just to have something to do.

She didn't have to wait long, because the door opened and Case stepped into the cafe with all the self-assurance she'd admired in him yesterday. He was no longer covered in dots of dough, sprinkles of cookie toppings, and a dusting of flour. He looked fresh-scrubbed and clean shaven, but the sparkle in his eye told her he wasn't all that different from the dangerous-looking man who'd stepped off the Harley.

"I hope your coffee is still hot," she said as he sat down.

"I'm sure it's fine. I'd rather have a glass of milk, but I think my aunt believes I've outgrown that particular drink."

"You have to admit, it doesn't fit with your ... image."

"My image," he said carefully, taking a sip from the mug. "What do you mean?"

Mandy had the impression she'd somehow offended him. "Perhaps I used the wrong word. I shouldn't have made assumptions."

"That I was a biker dude?" he said with some humor in his deep voice.

Mandy nodded. "First impressions are hard to break."

"True. But I'd been on the road for three days, and shaving wasn't a top priority. The whiskers give me some protection against those pesky sixty-five mile per hour bugs."

She smiled. "Would I be too nosy if I asked where you'd come from?"

"Not at all. Just outside Denver. I live not too far from Estes Park."

"So now you're a mountain man as well?"

Case chuckled. "I suppose you could say that. Or maybe you should keep an open mind. I might surprise you."

Oh, you already have, Mandy wanted to say. "I wasn't

judging, but I have to admit that I tend to categorize people."

"Rather like a human Dewey Decimal System?"

Mandy smiled, then nodded. "Yes, I suppose so."

By mutual unspoken agreement, both of them reached for their muffins. Case added a pat of butter, but Mandy ate hers plain. Splurging on a large muffin was all the calories she needed. Without a health club in town, she had to rely on walking and some exercises at home to stay in shape. And that meant even more self-discipline.

"These are very good," she said after swallowing a mouthful. "You're a great baker."

"I'll tell you a little secret," he said, leaning forward. "It's not hard when you have your aunt telling you everything to do. If she's not here tomorrow, then I'm not going to guarantee quality or quantity."

Mandy smiled, enjoying breakfast despite her earlier nervousness. Case Gardner was a study in contrasts, and she still didn't know quite what to think of him. She did know, however, that she was spending entirely too much time thinking *about* him.

Millicent bustled over and refilled their coffee cups, smiling as she looked back and forth between the two of them. "Are you having a good breakfast?" she asked, innocently enough.

"Yes, Aunt Millie."

"Yes, thank you."

Her grin widened. "If you need anything, just let me know," she said as she fluttered back behind the counter.

"My aunt is matchmaking," Case said just as Mandy took the last bite of her muffin.

She choked, clapping a hand over her mouth as

she struggled for control. Case quickly retrieved a glass of water from the counter and handed it to her.

"Should I pound on your back?"

Mandy shook her head, her eyes watering as the coughs subsided.

"I'm sorry. I thought you knew."

She took a sip from the glass. "I . . . I wasn't sure. I mean, I didn't want to presume—"

"That Millicent believes we'd make a great couple?" he finished for her.

Mandy nodded, too surprised to say much to his blunt comments.

"Why do you think they sent me to the library before I'd even unpacked my duffel bag? They couldn't wait for me to meet you."

"Really?" Mandy tried to sound only mildly interested, but knew she'd failed when his eyes twinkled in merriment.

"I wasn't sure what to expect. After all, I remember the old—or should I say former—librarian."

"Mrs. Crabtree," Mandy said, recalling the stern-faced woman who'd run the old library with military control.

"Since I was only here during the summers, I just wanted to have a good time. It's a wonder that woman didn't spoil all libraries for me forever."

"I take it she didn't?"

"No, I still love the smell of a library, the feel of a well-bound book, and bookstores. They're all great."

"I spent a lot of time in the library when I was young, too," she admitted, thinking of her mother, who hadn't valued books as much as she had life experience. Mandy knew she wouldn't have gone to college, much less obtained her master's degree in

Library Science, if she hadn't loved learning so much. Of course, she hadn't always been the greatest student . . .

"So how did you end up in Scottsville? You didn't grow up around here, did you?"

"No, I didn't." And she wasn't ready to talk about her personal life, either. "Look at the time!" she said, glancing quickly at the sensible, large-numbered watch on her wrist. "I need to get to the library."

"I thought you weren't open yet."

"I'm trying to set a regular schedule. If anyone comes in, I'll see if we can help."

"Do I make you nervous, Mandy Thompson?" Case asked, his voice lower, more intimate. He leaned forward, his hand lightly covering hers. Despite the morning sunlight outside and the bright fluorescent lights overhead, the restaurant atmosphere suddenly changed from bakery to bistro, from serene to seductive.

"No . . . I . . . I just need to go."

"You're not good at fibbing."

"I don't know what you mean," she said, pushing back her chair and abruptly standing.

Case rose with long-limbed ease and predatory grace, his smile making her think of long nights rather than early mornings. "I'll see you later."

"I thought you were working at the bakery."

"We close at two o'clock," he said, folding his arms across his chest. "And I remember what you said about needing help."

"I didn't mean—"

"Don't worry," he said, stopping her by raising his hand. "I'm not going to show up to disrupt your carefully planned day. However, I might have some fundraising ideas.''

"Perhaps you should meet with the Friends of the Library committee," she suggested lamely, looping her combination purse and briefcase over her shoulder.

"Oh, but I need to run my ideas by you first. I'm sure you can give me a much better picture of your wants and needs.''

"My what?'' She nearly stumbled backward toward the door, the chair wobbling as she kicked the leg with her shoe's heavy sole. Surely he hadn't just said what she thought he'd said!

"The library's wants and needs, of course,'' he clarified with an intimate smile that caused her heart to beat faster.

"Good day, Mr. Gardner," she said as she took off, thankful for her sensible shoes. "Thank you, Millicent,'' she said as she escaped out the door of the Gardner Bakery.

"Goodbye, dear,'' Millicent said as Mandy retreated to the safety of her library.

Case watched her hasty flight down the cracked, uneven sidewalk, around the town square, and toward the street where her sanctuary awaited. With another smile and a shake of his head, he turned back to the counter.

His aunt was watching him, her gray penciled eyebrows raised nearly to her lavender-tinted hair.

"I think she likes me," he said with a shrug of his shoulders.

CHAPTER THREE

There was no way she could afford to buy a computer system for the library, Mandy realized with a sigh as she studied the row of numbers one more time. As much as she wanted to modernize the library, the small town budget simply didn't have the funds for a computer network. That meant completing a new card catalog for the salvaged books, since the old cards were smoke-damaged. And that also meant a lot of hours for some volunteers using outdated typewriters instead of state-of-the-art software.

She tucked the paper inside her desk drawer and leaned her chin on her hand. It was near closing time and there was no one in the makeshift library. Afternoon sunlight streamed in the wide windows, sending dust motes dancing and warming the former bookstore to summertime temperatures. Mandy yawned, a testament to her restless night.

"Thanks to Case Gardner," she mumbled, resisting

the urge to fold her arms and lay her head down on the smooth oak of the old desk. A short nap would be heavenly, but she'd probably end up sleeping through closing time and maybe on into the evening. The lone patrolman would find her alone in the unlocked library sometime around ten o'clock, she speculated.

That type of behavior just wasn't appropriate. She might as well close up for the day.

She grabbed her briefcase, stuffed the papers inside, and fished out her keys. A brisk walk home was just what she needed to clear her mind of wayward thoughts. Plus, she'd be wide awake by the time she arrived home. Tonight, she'd broil a chicken breast for dinner and steam some nice healthy vegetables.

Just what she needed.

Except her mouth watered for something a little more spicy and little more forbidden.

And a whole lot more masculine.

She held her chin high and took a deep breath. She had to stop thinking about Case Gardner immediately. He was just passing through. Okay, maybe he was kind to come and help out his aunts. Or maybe he was just hanging out because he didn't have a regular job. He could have gotten kicked out of his residence in Colorado. Maybe his girlfriend had given him the boot. That would be a really good explanation for his arrival in town.

Normal men didn't just take off and help their elderly relatives. They might send some money or help hire someone to care for them, but they didn't ride their motorcycle for three days and then move in.

How could he afford that big, new motorcycle, anyway?

Shrugging off the persistent yet inappropriate questions, Mandy marched down the sidewalk toward the town square, the soles of her sensible shoes making no sound on the aging concrete.

She'd just taken a few steps down the walkway leading to her house when an exotic yet familiar rumble disturbed the quiet afternoon.

Case Gardner on his Harley.

With an iron will, she forced herself not to react to the thrill she felt at that realization.

He roared to a stop, the front forks just a foot or so from the rounded toes of her shoes, the wheel blocking her path.

She raised her chin, took a deep breath, and mentally prepared herself to chastise him for acting more like a high school student than a full-grown man. When she looked into his eyes, however, all her well intentioned plans fluttered to the ground like the crumbs of a two-day-old muffin.

"Good afternoon, Mandy," he said in a deep sexy voice that sent shivers down her spine.

"I was just on my way home, if you'd please move your motorcycle."

"I went by the library," he said, as if she hadn't just asked him to perform a simple act of courtesy, "to see if I could help you out. I didn't notice the hours yesterday."

"There's no sense staying open late when we have no patrons. Besides, I have work to do at home," she said, holding up her briefcase.

He made a tsk-tsk sound, shaking his head as

though she had said something horrible. "All work and no play. Haven't you heard that's bad for you?"

She realized she was trapped between him, the motorcycle, and the picket fence to her back . . . and the thought unnerved her.

"Why are you doing this?" she asked in a voice just above a whisper.

"Doing what?" He was so close she could smell his aftershave and soap. So close she could see the flecks of gold in his green eyes.

"Following me." She looked at him directly, summoning outrage so that she wouldn't grab hold of his lightweight sweater and pull him even closer.

"Is that what you think I'm doing?" he said, amusement fading from his voice as his eyes darkened. "Actually I just happened to be driving down this street. And there you were."

Had the sun gone in? Suddenly, Mandy felt as though they were all alone, as though the rest of the world—even nature—had deserted them. The wind didn't blow, nor could she hear any birds singing.

The pounding rush of blood through her body, on the other hand, sounded deafening.

"Well, now you know where I live."

"So I do," he said simply.

"Case . . . what do you want?" She had a strong inclination to be even ruder and rush to the safety of her tidy little house. But the wild part of her wanted to jump behind him on the powerful motorcycle, throw her arms around him, and ride off into the sunset.

Case studied her for a moment.

"Say you'll have dinner with me."

"I have work to do," she said. She knew he wouldn't believe the evasive response.

"I won't keep you out too late. We'll just have a little dinner and a little conversation." He leaned even closer until she saw the small dark freckle above his left eyebrow and the tiny scar on his chin. "You're not afraid of me, are you?"

"Of course I'm not afraid of you! I just—well, I just can't."

"Any particular reason why?"

"I've already told you."

"Yes," he said, his eyes raking over her from the top of her smoothly styled hair to the toes of her walking shoes. "I guess you have."

He couldn't possibly have noticed anything interesting, since she'd very carefully dressed to camouflage any signs of a figure. She would have done that anyway, but today, since she'd known she was going to see him at the bakery, she had wanted to make sure she didn't give him any encouragement.

"The question is, why are you trying so hard to avoid me?"

"Wha . . . what do you mean?" Surely he didn't know the temptation he presented. He couldn't understand how she struggled to be productive in a world that offered so many diversions.

"I mean," Case said softly, reaching out and fingering a strand of hair that brushed against her jaw, "that the more you hide, the more I wonder what's underneath that disguise."

She straightened her spine, trying not to melt into a puddle right there on the town square. "I'm not wearing a disguise." Her voice sounded husky, as though she was coming down with something,

Like a bad case of lust, a little voice informed her.

"Yes, you are." He tugged on her hair, pulling her closer.

She felt her eyes widen as her breath caught in her throat. Fear made her swallow, breaking the seductive pull of his gold-flecked eyes.

"Don't you dare kiss me, Case Gardner."

Case stared at Mandy's inviting lips for just a moment too long. She jerked back, making a tiny sound of distress as she came up against the fence. When he looked into her eyes, he saw a combination of fear and excitement.

He hadn't wanted to frighten her, but he couldn't ignore the sense of triumph that surged through his body when he realized she wanted him—perhaps as much as he wanted her.

She just wasn't ready to admit it yet.

With a sigh of resignation, he stepped back, letting her escape. "I guess you really don't want to go to dinner tonight," he said casually, trying to ease out of the awkward situation with his pride intact.

"I think it would be best if we didn't get involved . . . in that manner." Her voiced sounded breathy, as though she'd been walking briskly for a long way in those damn ugly shoes.

"I only offered dinner, Mandy," he said as he swung his leg over the Harley, "not breakfast, too."

She drew herself up, her full lips forming a thin line. She took a deep breath, pressing her breasts against the baggy, shapeless form of her dress. But when she opened her mouth, no sound came forth. Instead, she frowned, walked around the back of the motorcycle, and said crisply, "Good afternoon, Mr. Gardner."

Case smiled, then started the engine. The big bike purred beneath him like a well-satisfied woman. Not exactly the mental image he wanted at the moment.

He rolled away from the sidewalk, then shadowed her as she walked quickly down the residential street.

Pulling alongside, he said, "Have a nice evening, Miss Mandy. We can go out to dinner another time."

"As I said, I don't think that's a good idea."

"But I'm a persistent guy. It's my goal to change your mind."

"I'm a woman of high principles," she said in a haughty voice that would have done any nineteenth-century schoolmarm proud.

Case chuckled. "I'm not talking about principles, Mandy. I'm talking about having fun. You know— laughing, enjoying each other's company, making out on a cool night. The rest is up to you."

"It's *all* up to me, Mr. Gardner," she said, stopping and giving him a stern look. "And the answer is no."

Case stretched his back, took a deep breath, and gave her a once-over that was so obvious she couldn't miss the implication. "I'll get you to say yes, Miss Mandy. The only mystery is this: What will the question be?"

Before she could sputter and stamp, he gunned the engine and took off.

Case spent the next two days learning more about the bakery, relieving Millicent of many of the duties she'd assumed since Greta's accident. He also set up a box for donated books, urging the bakery's regular patrons to bring new and used books in for the library.

A stroke of genius, he told himself. Mandy wouldn't be able to ignore him when he arrived with a sizeable library donation. To sweeten the pot, he made a phone call to New York. With any luck, by the beginning of next week, he'd have a real good reason to spend time at the library. And she'd go out to dinner with him, because she'd have a good excuse to give in to her natural curiosity about him, not to mention exploring the attraction that only he was ready to admit.

During mornings at the bakery, he became reacquainted with many of the townspeople he'd known as a child. He soon realized that his duties included taking time to talk and gossip, especially in the hours between breakfast and lunch. Millicent urged him to pour himself a cup of coffee and have a few cookies or a muffin while he chatted with the Scottsville residents.

If he wasn't careful, he was going to roll out of town on his own, he thought, rubbing his still flat stomach. He needed a gym, but without one, some hard labor would do. Unfortunately, the heaviest thing he'd been required to lift was a ten-pound sack of flour.

Mandy didn't come to the bakery on Tuesday, prompting speculation from Millicent that the librarian might have a cold. *Cold feet was more like it,* Case thought. Mandy did stop by briefly on Wednesday morning, just long enough to grab a cup of coffee and a muffin to go. He'd seen her only long enough to say "good morning" before she bolted out the door, full skirt swishing just above her sensible shoes.

Damn. Nuns showed more leg than Mandy Thompson.

On Wednesday afternoon, he drove Greta to her doctor, using his aunts' Buick. The car was one of the land-yacht models, with wide bench seats and lots of leg room. He would have loved this car when he was a teenager, he thought, gripping the wheel with both hands. What a great place to make out.

As soon as that thought popped into his head, an image of Mandy materialized. She'd kick off those ugly shoes, curl her legs beneath her, and settle back against the seat. He'd scoot over, pull her closer, and make quick work of her equally ugly dress. At least the darn thing was baggy enough to get her out of it fairly easily.

"Case, were you listening? You need to take this exit."

He inhaled, blinked several times, and focused on the present. "Sorry, Aunt Greta. I was just enjoying your car."

"I imagine it seems very nice compared to that loud motorcycle of yours."

"It's certainly different," he said noncommittally, knowing his aunts would never understand the fun of riding a powerful bike across the wide open spaces. He'd owned a lot of vehicles, but the new Harley had to be one of his favorites.

He wondered if Mandy liked motorcycles. She'd eyed the big bike with a mixture of fascination and dread, much like she'd looked at him.

"If you ever want to use the car, just let us know. I won't be driving it for quite some time, and Millicent doesn't need to go out much."

He gently slowed onto the exit ramp, then pulled

to a stop at the intersection. "Thanks, Aunt Greta, but I doubt I'll need a car while I'm in town."

"Well," she said thoughtfully, "you might if you were to go on a date, for example."

"A date," he said, wondering if his aunt could read minds. He turned left and headed south into Tyler.

"Yes. For example, if you were to take Mandy Thompson out to dinner at that new catfish restaurant near Gladewater, a car would come in handy."

He glanced at his aunt, only to find her staring innocently ahead at the traffic on the state highway.

"So you think I should ask Mandy to dinner?" he asked carefully.

"She's an attractive young lady. I would understand if you might like to spend some time with her."

He remembered Mandy's prim refusal, and grinned.

"But do you think a very proper young woman like her would want to go out with an improper guy like me?"

"Oh, don't be silly. I know perfectly well that you've gone out of your way to make her believe you're little better than a bum. Why, those whiskers of yours wouldn't have been tolerated in my day." Greta held up her hand when he started to smile. "Now, I know times have changed. I watch television, you know. Women nowadays seem to think that scruffy look is sexy."

"You think Mandy finds me sexy?" he asked, still smiling.

Greta nodded.

CHAPTER FOUR

"Mandy, this is Case."

She held the cordless phone in a white-knuckled grip, her heart beating faster at the sound of his voice.

Boy, she had it bad.

"Mandy? Are you there?"

"I'm here," she said finally.

Before she could tell him to get lost, he continued. "I still want to go out to dinner with you. Have you thought any more about accepting my invitation?"

Only every waking hour, she wanted to say. "I . . . I still don't think that would be a good idea."

"I think it would be a great idea. I'm really a nice guy. Ask my aunts. They're totally impartial."

Mandy had to smile. "I'm sure they are. But—"

But nothing. If she didn't end this call, she might say yes. Quickly, she unlatched the screen door, reached around the door facing, held the cordless

phone inside the house with one arm, and rang the
doorbell.

She snatched the phone back to her ear. "Case,
I'm sorry. Someone's at the door. I have to go."

"I'll hold," he offered.

"No, I'm sure it's a neighbor. I may be a while."
For good measure, she reached around and rang the
bell again. "I really have to go. Talk to you later.

With a punch of the button, she hung up and let
out a deep breath. How horribly sneaky of her. She'd
actually lied, all because she couldn't face the prospect of going out with him, getting on his motorcycle,
wrapping her arms around his waist, and holding on
for dear life as he roared off into the night.

Mandy sighed, wishing it were easier to tell him
no. Case had only been in town four days, and she
was already thinking about him much too much.

But she wasn't that kind of girl . . . no, make that
woman. She was sensible and strong, and she wouldn't
be swayed by a great smile and the best body she'd
seen in a month of Sundays.

All she had to find was a really great excuse to
keep Case at bay. Unfortunately, her imagination had
never been very good at coming up with reasons *not*
to do something that sounded like a whole lot of fun.

He watched her from the doorway as she talked to
a middle-aged woman who was dressed less conserva-
tively than Mandy. Both women held cups of coffee
in their hands, obviously enjoying some light refresh-
ments before the meeting began.

Why did Mandy hide herself inside baggy, old-lady
dresses and boxy shoes? Granted, she could possibly

have some kind of foot problem that necessitated orthopedic footwear, but he'd seen her in jeans and a sweater in a photo on his aunts' bulletin board. There was nothing wrong with her figure. The more he saw her hiding in those shapeless dresses, the more he longed to run his hands over her curves and hollows.

But standing in the doorway of the city council chamber where the Friends of the Library met, lusting after the librarian, wasn't doing anything but making his jeans tight. Case put a smile on his face, balanced the box in front of him, and walked into the room.

The informal chatter faltered and faded away. Mandy looked up from her conversation. Her gaze met his and he felt the pull of attraction, even in such a public setting.

"Case . . . Mr. Gardner. What are you doing here?"

Her voice gave away her confusion over his appearance, but also hinted at her excitement. She wasn't really upset to see him. His polite smile turned into a genuine one.

"We've been collecting books at the bakery," he explained, setting the box down on the table. "I have some more in the car."

"Car?"

"My aunts were kind enough to let me borrow theirs."

"I see." She turned to the woman standing beside her. "I'm sorry. Where are my manners? Mrs. Wilkins, this is Case Gardner, Greta and Millicent's nephew."

"Oh, I've met Case," Mrs. Wilkins said, her expression showing that she wasn't too old to look—not that he considered himself handsome. Still, he knew his looks made him interesting to women, which was fine with him.

Especially when one of the interested women was Mandy Thompson.

"Nice to see you again, Mrs. Wilkins," he said. He lifted a tray of goodies out of the box. "I hope you see some of your favorites here. I made most of these myself." He removed the protective wrap and placed the tray on the table, near the coffee pot.

"Really?" She leaned forward at the variety of cookies and small scones from the bakery. Case gazed at Mandy, who seemed to be even more confused. He imagined she wanted to ask what he was doing here, but she was too polite to do such a thing, particularly in front of an audience.

Although he was still suspicious of the sudden interruption to their phone call last night.

The other four members of the Friends of the Library board gathered around, saying hello and picking their favorite treats to go with their coffee. Mandy didn't choose anything, but she did frown at him while everyone else was busy.

He pulled her aside. "Don't frown. You'll cause so many wrinkles that people will believe you're old enough to be wearing those dresses."

"There's nothing wrong with my clothing," she said defensively, using that huffy tone he found so endearing. She drew herself up as tall as possible, as though she might be able to intimidate him into leaving—or at least stop his teasing.

"Not if you're eighty, I suppose. But I didn't come by to critique your wardrobe."

"No? Then why did you come by?"

"I told you, I like books. I'm just supporting the community effort."

Mandy frowned. "Why do I have a hard time believing you?"

"Maybe because you're too suspicious. Just relax, Mandy. I'm not up to some nefarious purpose."

"I—"

"Mandy, we're ready to begin," Mrs. Wilkins interrupted.

"Of course." Mandy gave him a forced smile as she turned to take her seat. Case decided not to publicly bait her. He poured himself a cup of coffee, then walked two rows back and chose a seat at an angle where he could watch her unobserved.

The secretary read the minutes of their last meeting, and then Mrs. Wilkins, obviously the president of the group, gave an update on their fundraising efforts. Case found their efforts admirable, but inadequate to furnish the new library that was being created in a former business location on the town square.

Millicent had shown him the two-story structure where the contractor was replacing warped floors and building shelves into the new walls. The insurance settlement from the fire would cover the construction and replacement of many of the books, but not all that needed to be done. They'd told him the old library hadn't changed since he was a boy visiting Scottsville. That meant everything was woefully out of date.

As he sipped his coffee, he listened quietly as they finalized plans for a bake sale at the upcoming Autumn Festival. From what he could tell, the town event put a different title on what was just another

Halloween party. Scottsville, he supposed, was trying to be politically correct.

"Have you tried to get authors to come to town for a book signing?" he asked when they finished discussing the bake sale.

"We have a number of authors in East Texas, but I don't see how we could make much money with a book signing," Mandy said when the rest of the board remained silent.

"Why is that?"

"Because we'd have to buy the books, or get a bookstore to order them and maybe give us a portion of the profit. We might also incur expenses from getting authors to come to town."

"Have you tried to get books donated by publishers?"

"We sent out letters asking for donations to replenish the shelves," she answered, some irritation showing in her voice. Case had a feeling she'd really like him to shut up and go home.

"But how about if you could get publishers to donate books and the authors to sign them? If you didn't have any expenses, wouldn't that be a good fundraiser?"

"I suppose, but I'm not sure how to set something like that up."

"Would it be okay with the board if I made a few calls? I have some connections."

Mandy opened her mouth to say something, but then apparently thought better of it. Mrs. Wilkins jumped in, however, and said, "That would be just fine, Case. If you can make those calls, why don't you get back to us at our next meeting? When is that,

Florence?" the president asked, turning to another woman on the board.

"October 22, about a week before the Harvest Festival."

"Will that give you enough time?"

"Sure. As a matter of fact, if I get some good news before then, I might just pass that along to Ms. Thompson, if that's all right with the board."

"I'm sure that would be fine," Mrs. Wilkins said, giving a smile and a nod to Mandy.

Mandy forced a smile on her face, but when she turned back, she was frowning.

"Wrinkles," he whispered, pointing to his own forehead.

She set her lips in a thin line, took a deep breath, and turned back to face the front of the room.

Case settled back in his chair and smiled. He'd just created another reason to spend time with Miss Mandy Thompson.

Mandy gathered her papers and her appointment book, ready to rush out with the rest of the board. She would do anything to keep from being alone with Case. She knew he'd planned his departure to get her alone. She could see it in his dark, compelling eyes as he watched her from the doorway. He smiled and shook hands with everyone else, but he wasn't really looking at them.

A shiver raced through her body. What would he do if he caught her? Would his hands skim over her, as hot as his seductive gaze? Would his lips claim hers with passion and possession like she'd never felt before?

A sigh escaped her as she hugged her paperwork close. She had to get out of here right now. If she was alone with Case, there was no telling what she might do, from encouraging his interest to jumping his large, muscular body. She needed to get away quickly, but he'd just said goodnight to the last of the board members except for Mrs. Wilkins, who was unplugging the coffee pot and covering the goodies Case had brought.

"Take those with you, Mrs. Wilkins," he offered with a smile. "I certainly don't need more cookies."

His remarks made the board president laugh, but all Mandy could think of was getting out the door, stride for stride with Mrs. Wilkins and the tray of cookies.

She almost made it. He gathered the donated books into one box, then held the door open for them, politely asking if they needed any help out to their cars. Mandy mumbled a quick "no" and stayed close to the older woman as she locked up for the night. Mrs. Wilkins thanked him for coming and continued to her car.

"Mandy, wait," Case said before she could make a clean escape. "I have another box of books for the library."

She stood there on the sidewalk and watched Mrs. Wilkins unlock her car, wave once, and slip inside the vehicle.

Mandy sighed, wondering if she had the strength to resist Case Gardner on a crisp autumn night, with the smell of wood smoke and rustling leaves filling the air.

"Mandy?"

She turned, focusing on his pale denim shirt that seemed to glow in the moonlight and shadows. "Yes?"

"Would you like for me to take these to the library for you?"

She should say no. Being alone with him on a public street was tempting enough, but to invite him into the darkened library would be plain foolish. Her will-power wasn't that strong, not when faced with such temptation.

"If it's not too inconvenient," she heard herself say.

"Good. Did you drive to the meeting?"

"Yes." She nodded toward her yellow compact car two spaces down. "You can follow me over."

"I'll be right behind you," he said in a sexy voice that caused another shiver to run through her body. Good grief, why couldn't she keep her mind out of the gutter?

She had to try three times before she finally inserted the key into the ignition. On the short drive to the library, she glanced several times into the rearview mirror. The bright headlights of Greta and Millicent's enormous Buick were right behind her, as promised. No one else was out and about, and she felt as though she and Case were the only two people on earth.

Her heart rate picked up as she rolled to a stop in front of the temporary library. She cut her lights, and Case pulled in beside her and did the same. With no engines running, the night seemed suddenly silent. The building just off the square was dark and deserted.

"Don't be silly," she whispered to herself as she popped a red cinnamon breath mint into her dry mouth. She seemed determined to make more out of this simple transfer of books than the situation warranted.

When Case tapped on her window, she practically jumped through the roof of her car. Closing her eyes briefly and telling herself to get control of her pounding heart, she grasped the door handle and pulled.

The scent of pine and fallen leaves was stronger here than at city hall, but the breeze also carried Case's clean, crisp fragrance. She inhaled, telling herself that she wasn't imprinting his scent to call up later, when she lay alone in bed. She told herself that she didn't want to bury her face against his chest and hold on tight.

"It's cool out tonight," he said, shielding her from the brisk wind with his body as he leaned against the open car door.

"Yes, it is." Had they really resorted to talking about the weather? Perhaps he didn't feel the same attraction she was experiencing.

Nonsense. He'd made his intentions perfectly clear, just as she'd consistently rebuffed his advances. Only at the moment, she didn't feel much like saying "no." Why was that?

Stupidity, she felt like answering. And a sudden urge to throw away all caution.

To hide her confusion, she grabbed her keys and slid out of the driver's seat. "Do you need any help carrying in the boxes?" She didn't spare a glance at his face because she was afraid of what she'd find— a mixture of sexy amusement and glowing desire.

"No, I think I can manage."

He didn't move, so she was forced to brush against him as she walked toward the entrance of the library.

The contact felt more intimate than many embraces, even though he didn't try to touch or crowd her. She glanced up, making eye contact for one charged instant. If she didn't move now, he was going to kiss her.

She broke away, scooting past him faster than the strong autumn breeze that blew fallen leaves against her bare ankles. Fumbling with the keys, she finally found the right one and turned the lock. From behind her, she heard the trunk lid slam shut.

Pushing open the door, she searched for the light switch. Funny, but she could have sworn it was right here on the wall.

Case brushed past her, his leg grazing her hips. The box bumped against her back, jostling her hand on the wall.

"Sorry," he said softly, finding the counter even in the near darkness. How could he see so well when she couldn't even find the light switch she'd used a hundred times?

"Mandy?"

"Yes?" she said in a husky voice that didn't sound like her own.

She felt his hands on her upper arms, then sliding lower as he pressed himself against her back. He was warm and solid, but still she shivered.

"Are you cold?"

"No."

"You're shivering."

"You make me nervous."

"Good nervous or bad nervous?"

She tried to turn, but his arms tightened, pulling her close to his hard chest with her arms crossed just under her breasts. "How can nervous be good?" she whispered.

"Maybe it's not nerves you're feeling. Did you think of that?"

All the time, she wanted to reply, but that would be telling him too much. She'd told enough fibs, all in the name of proper behavior and decorum. So she nodded, brushing her hair against his chin with the movement.

He bent his head lower until she felt his warm breath on her neck. His arms tightened, and suddenly she seemed unable to breathe. She realized it wasn't because of his embrace. The restriction came from within, from a heart-pounding sense of anticipation.

His lips grazed her skin and she trembled. His breath skimmed along her skin and a ripple of sensation traveled outward like the waves of a pebble thrown into still water.

She moaned, closing her eyes against the wickedly intense feeling of his sensual kisses. How she wanted to turn around and feel his lips on hers, to experience the overwhelming possession of their first kiss.

But Case Gardner seemed intent on going slow. He released her wrists, only to stroke her waist, her arms, and her shoulders. His mouth moved gently from beneath her ear to the neckline of her dress, until his breathing grew as heavy as hers.

"Kiss me," she whispered.

"I thought you'd never ask," he mumbled against her jaw.

CHAPTER FIVE

Case turned her quickly, before she had a chance to remember all the reasons they shouldn't be kissing. She had a dozen, but he had a far more compelling argument—the force of their desire.

Her slender body molded to his as though they'd been created only for each other. The weak light from outside bathed her ivory skin in a silvery glow and showed her parted lips to perfection.

A perfection he could resist no longer.

His lips settled over hers. She tasted of cinnamon and sugar, her lips so soft he nearly lost control. After a moment of hesitation, she opened to him.

He slanted his mouth across hers, stroked her, their breath merging into one. Mandy felt so good in his arms, so very right. How had he lived all these years without tasting her sweetness?

How could he . . . no, he wouldn't think of that

right now. Not when she was warm and willing in his arms.

"Mandy," he murmured as he lifted his lips. He tried to see her face in the dim light, but couldn't read her expression. Her eyes were nearly closed, her lips damp and parted, her cheeks flushed. He'd never seen such a beautiful sight.

"You're incredible," he whispered against her lips before the next delicious kiss.

One hand skimmed low to mold over her hips. She moaned, but didn't pull away. Her rear was firm, just as he'd imagined. He pressed her close, needing to feel her against his arousal, needing her to know what she did to him.

Her arms circled his neck, her hands tangled through his hair and stroked his shoulders, arousing him even more. He wondered where they could find space to lie down in the jumble of temporary shelving and partially unpacked boxes.

Hell, it didn't matter. Standing up against the wall would do just fine. He turned them and moved her backward against the first hard, stationary surface he could find.

The jolt of connecting with the wall seemed to surprise Mandy. She broke the kiss and looked up at him with startled, passion-glazed eyes.

"What are you doing?" she whispered.

"Kissing you senseless," he answered, lowering his mouth to her waiting lips.

"Senseless," she repeated, avoiding his kiss. Her arms dropped from around his neck, one hand rubbing her forehead.

The other pushed against his chest.

"What's wrong?" He was afraid he already knew the answer.

"I can't believe I . . . that we . . ."

"Almost made love standing up?" he finished for her.

He swore he could feel the heat of her blush across the rapidly increasing space that separated them.

"No! We didn't almost do anything." She pressed her fingers to her temples as she turned away from him. "I can't believe I let you—"

"Let me?" he interrupted. "Who asked me to kiss her just a few minutes ago?"

"Okay, maybe more than 'let you,' " she conceded, rubbing harder, as though she could avoid a headache by vigorous action.

Not the action he would have chosen, he thought as he narrowed his eyes in frustration. "Mandy, we haven't done anything wrong."

"Oh, that's easy for you to say," she said, beginning to pace the limited area of the library. "You've made your intentions perfectly clear."

"Yes, I have. You're the one that's a little confused." He tried to state the obvious observation gently, but heard an edge to his voice that he didn't like. He wasn't the kind of man to heap accusations on a woman or criticize her decisions. But, damn it, Mandy didn't seem to be able to decide. All he'd tried to do was help her make the right decision—to give in to the attraction, to see where it could lead.

Apparently, she didn't like the direction their relationship was headed.

"I'm not . . . okay, I was a little confused. But I'm not anymore. I've decided—"

He crossed the space separating them, placing a

finger across her lips before she could say another word. "Don't," he ordered gently. "Don't say something you'll regret later."

"I won't," she promised after pushing his hand away.

"Yes, you will. I have a feeling that once you take a stand, you just hate to back down. Or admit that you were wrong. Or change your mind." He smiled at her frustrated expression. "Let's just call it a night. Sleep on it, so to speak."

"That's not funny," she said, folding her arms across her chest.

Case shrugged. "Maybe not, but that's the best I can come up with at the moment."

"Case, this is crazy!"

"Maybe," he said, tracing the line of her cheekbone with one finger, "but I sure feel pretty sane at the moment." He smiled at her perplexed expression. "Frustrated, but entirely sane and lucid."

"Case," she chastised.

"Mandy," he mimicked, then chuckled when she practically stamped her foot. Before she could begin another explanation of why they shouldn't get involved, he lowered his head and took her lips in a quick but thorough kiss.

"Goodnight, Miss Mandy," he whispered against her parted lips. "We'll talk about this after you've had some time to think about how right that felt."

He walked to the door. "I'm going to the car now. I'm sitting there until you lock up and get into your own car. If you're not out of here in two minutes, I'm coming in after you."

"There's no reason to wait for me. This isn't the big city."

"Humor me," he said. "Deep down inside, I'm really a traditional kind of guy."

He left before she could laugh in his face or throw a book at him.

"Mandy, this is Case."

After not hearing his voice all day Friday, but thinking about him almost constantly, she wasn't really surprised that her heart started to tap dance as soon as he said her name. She ran her tongue over her dry lips, remembering all too well his passionate kisses.

"Mandy?"

"I'm here," she said finally, her voice sounding as though she'd just run a 5K race.

"You didn't come by the bakery this morning."

"I was running late."

"Oversleep?"

No, at least not until her alarm had awakened her from a fitful slumber. She'd spent most of the night tossing and turning, reliving each moment in Case's arms. When she had finally gone to sleep, she'd dreamed of his powerful kisses—and imagined much more. "Yes," she answered simply. "I overslept."

"I thought maybe you were avoiding me."

"No. Why would I do that?" she asked innocently, as though nothing unusual had happened the night before.

"Oh, no reason," he replied casually, with a trace of humor in his voice. "Does that mean that you're ready to go out with me?"

"On a date?" she squeaked.

"Yes, unless you'd like to make it more than that."

"What do you mean?"

"A weekend. I think I could arrange something, even on short notice."

"No! I mean, I hadn't . . . I wouldn't even consider . . . that."

"Oh? I'm disappointed that you're still frightened of me."

"I'm not frightened of you!"

"Okay. Prove it."

"I don't have to prove anything to you, Case Gardner," she said peevishly.

"Maybe you wouldn't be proving it to *me,*" he said softly.

"What? Oh, you are so sure of yourself, aren't you?" She paced the length of the kitchen, then marched down the hall. "I don't have to prove anything to *myself* either. I know how I feel."

"Do you? I still sense some hesitation. I'll bet you're pacing the floor right now, telling yourself you're certain when in reality—"

"That's all in your head." She pulled back the curtain at the front window, making sure he wasn't sitting at the curb talking on a cellular phone. She wouldn't put that past him, although those bills could get really expensive, and she still didn't know what Case did for a living when he wasn't working at his aunts' bakery.

Not that she'd asked . . .

"Have you thought about last night?" he asked in a soft bedroom voice that made her sag against the wall. The solid feel against her back reminded her again of the kisses they'd shared.

Oh, yes, she'd spent nearly every moment recalling last night in exquisite, torturous detail. "I've given it some thought."

"And what conclusions did you reach?"

"I don't really have an explanation for my actions. I can only say—"

"Don't you dare apologize for asking me to kiss you, Mandy Thompson," he growled into the phone.

"I . . . I wasn't going to apologize." *Liar,* her inner voice accused. *That's exactly what you were going to do.*

"Tell me you're not sorry," he asked.

"Case, please!" She didn't want to talk about what had happened between them. She certainly didn't want to admit her weakness for this totally inappropriate man.

"Case, please kiss me again?" he teased. "Is that what you meant?"

"You are being deliberately dense," she accused.

"I'm just trying to get you to admit how much you enjoyed last night." In a lower voice, he added, "And I don't mean the Friends of the Library Board meeting."

Mandy laughed in spite of herself. "Why are you always trying to make life difficult for me?"

"I didn't want to tell you this," he said in a stage whisper, "but I've been sent to Scottsville for that very reason. Working at the bakery is only my excuse. In fact, Greta even broke her ankle so I'd have a better reason to show up here and complicate your life."

"Case, you are incorrigible."

"Perhaps. Now, let's get back to my original question. Are you ready to go out with me?"

"I shouldn't, but I suppose you'll simply keep on making my life difficult until I say yes."

"I promise I'll be on my best behavior."

"Since I don't know you well enough to compare

that assurance to your regular behavior, I'm not so sure dinner would be a good idea."

"Mandy, Mandy, Mandy," he chastised, "you wound me, especially after last night. I'll have you know that I can behave myself very well when I want."

She smiled, then slipped into an overstuffed chair in her living room. Talking to him on the phone was so much easier than in person, where his dangerous good looks and tempting smiles made her struggle extra hard with her good intentions. "And would you want to be on your best behavior when we're at dinner?"

"Of course. I'd never embarrass you in public."

"That leads me to believe you would in private."

"I never tell all my secrets."

"You do seem to have a few."

The silence on the other end of the line was a telling reminder of how much she didn't know about this man. "What do you mean?" he asked.

"Just that I don't know what you do when you're not working in your aunts' bakery. For all I know, you could have a wife and kids back home in Colorado, or you might be running from the law."

"I promise you, I'm not wanted by any law enforcement agency. I'm not married now, nor have I ever been married, and I don't have any children. Although I'd be glad to discuss the issue with you in depth later."

Mandy blushed and smiled simultaneously. "You really are incorrigible. How can I take you seriously?"

"Why do you feel like you need to take me seriously?"

She had no ready answer to that simple question. At least, not one that she would reveal to a near-stranger, even if he was sexy and made her smile more than she had in ages.

"Mandy? Did I hit a nerve?"

"Maybe," she answered with a sigh. "I'm just not accustomed to starting any kind of a relationship— even a friendship—if I'm not sure there's some future in it."

She could practically hear him shrug. "Depends on what you call the future. I'm going to be here for at least two months while Greta mends. For some people, that's nearly a lifetime."

"I try to think a little farther into the future than that."

"Maybe you should try to live for the moment. You might discover a whole new world."

Discover? Rediscover was more like it. She had no desire to go back to the kind of life she used to lead in Dallas. "I'm not a spontaneous kind of person."

"I could teach you."

Oh, she had no doubt he'd try. But that would be like pouring gasoline on an already blazing fire. Before the night was over, she might just teach him a thing or two.

In fact, she could teach him things that weren't in the job description of small town librarian.

"Perhaps you'd be bored to death if we went out to dinner," she offered weakly.

"Don't be absurd. Just say you'll go and I'll show you I can be a charming date who will laugh at all your jokes and not even stare if you have spinach caught between your front teeth."

She laughed, then closed her eyes and sighed, feeling her resistance drain away. "All right," she said in a soft voice that she suspected he could barely hear. "I'll go out to dinner with you."

"You won't regret it," he said in that sexy, deep voice that promised so much more than sharing a meal. "How about tomorrow night?"

"I need to get up early on Sunday. I promised I'd fill in for an ailing member of the choir at church."

"I won't keep you out late. And we don't need to go far, if you'd rather not. Greta and Millicent told me about a new catfish restaurant near Gladewater, if you like catfish. That sounds casual."

"All right. As long as you promise not to keep me out late."

"Scout's honor."

"Tell me, Case Gardner," she said, laying her head on the chair's back, "were you ever a Boy Scout?"

"Of course," he said in an offended tone she suspected he was faking.

"I suppose you lived in a nice little house in the suburbs, attended Sunday School, and only terrorized your teachers on the last day of school."

He was quiet for a moment, then said, "You got most of it right."

"I—"

"So what time should I pick you up tomorrow? Since we have to get you home to bed early, how about six-thirty?"

He made the "getting her to bed" comment so casually that she couldn't call him on it, even though her own pulse kicked up another notch. "Six-thirty is fine."

"Then I'll see you then."

When she had given him directions to her house,

said goodbye and hung up the phone, she leaned back in her comfortable chair.

Had she done the right thing in agreeing to go out with him? Should she have tried harder to ignore the attraction between them? She wasn't sure. Perhaps she wouldn't know until after their date.

And if they had a good time, what then? More dates? More late night kisses and caresses that nearly set her on fire? A clandestine affair while he was in town for two months? She wasn't sure she could become involved with a fun-loving, outgoing man like Case and keep it a secret in a town as small as Scottsville.

She'd never tried to keep a secret like that before, just as she'd never known a man quite like him.

She could have understood his persistence more if she'd dressed suggestively, or flirted, or even acted more open to his attention. But she hadn't. She'd done everything she could think of to dissuade him from pursuing a relationship, and nothing had worked.

You didn't try hard enough, a little voice said. *You didn't try at all last night.*

Mandy sighed again, then heaved herself out of the chair. She'd better go check her closet for something to wear on a motorcycle date to a catfish restaurant. A flower-sprigged polyester blend jumper and white, lace-collared blouse hardly seemed appropriate.

Mandy worked with renewed vigor, unpacking the last of the books and stacking them neatly in the appropriate sections. The library patrons who came by buoyed her spirits, making her remember how important the library was to the community, and how much they needed to upgrade to a modern system. She especially loved to watch the faces of the children as they carefully made each selection. She wished the library could afford all the Newbery Award winners, plus the featured selections in the *Library Journal*. But without more funds, they would have to make do with five to ten year old books that the brothers and sisters of these children had already read a dozen times.

"There's nothing wrong with the classics," she told herself as she straightened up after the last patrons left. A glance at her watch confirmed closing time was only minutes away. She'd kept her mind on her job most of the day, but now that she needed to leave the sanctuary of the library, her thoughts turned to her dinner date with Case.

Case. Even his name caused her to sigh like a lovesick schoolgirl. How had this happened? She hadn't been this distracted by a guy since Chad Weston had transferred to her high school and driven the girls wild with his sexy swagger and pec-hugging T-shirts.

Was she still so shallow that a great body turned her brain to mush? No, in all honesty, she couldn't compare Chad to Case. The teenager hadn't possessed much more than good looks, while Case's intelligence and sense of humor complimented his other assets.

She might have a bad case of lust at first sight, but she also admired his dedication to his aunts, his sense of community, and his many other traits that she didn't have time to list if she was going to be on time for their date tonight.

After one last walk through the library to make

sure a small patron wasn't hiding in the stacks, Mandy switched off the lights, gathered her keys, and closed the door. She checked her watch; only an hour and a half until her date with Case. Taking a deep breath and pressing a hand to her fluttering heart, she set off at a brisk pace for home.

Case pulled the land yacht to a stop by the curb, cut the engine, and simply looked through the darkness for a few moments at Mandy's house before walking to the front door and ringing the bell. He hadn't been this nervous since he'd asked Christy McClelland to the prom.

He also hadn't agonized as much over what to wear since he'd simply rented a tuxedo for that event. Fortunately, tonight his selections had involved nothing more exotic than chinos versus jeans and a denim shirt versus a fisherman's sweater. Still, he wanted to make a good impression on Mandy for their first official date. He'd settled on a good pair of jeans and a freshly laundered denim shirt that Millicent had insisted on ironing for him.

He hoped Mandy would approve. He hadn't brought too many changes of clothing with him in his duffel bag.

"You're acting like an idiot," he mumbled to himself as he opened the car door. Besides, Mandy would probably be wearing one of her prim little dresses.

She'd left the light on for him, and a gusty wind blew brown and gold leaves across her front yard as he walked towards the door. Neatly banded flower beds contained some hardy flowers, and their orange and yellow blooms bobbed in the damp breeze.

Good thing he'd brought the car instead of the Harley. Riding a motorcycle in this weather could get real uncomfortable, especially if the predicted rain started before he got Mandy home. She seemed fascinated by his bike, but her interest would turn to disgust if she had to ride thirty miles in a cold rain.

An old-fashioned screen door gave more evidence of the traditional nature of Mandy's house and yard— as if he needed any after seeing her wardrobe, he thought with a smile. He was still smiling when he rang the doorbell.

She answered almost immediately, opening the door wide. Apparently, she'd been watching him, perhaps from the time he'd pulled up in front of her house.

He'd expected her to dress in something prissy, but her nubby green sweater and crisp jeans looked . . . great.

He was just about to tell her so when she blurted out, "You didn't bring the Harley."

He looked around at his aunts' large sedan. "No, I thought you'd be more comfortable in the car."

"Oh." She frowned just a little, then composed her features. "Of course."

"You're disappointed." He was surprised. He'd assumed she wouldn't want to ride on the back of the Harley in the darkness.

"No," she claimed, grabbing her purse from a table beside the door. "A car is much more practical, especially in this weather." With one fluid movement, she shut the door and locked it.

They were standing close together, but she obviously hadn't realized that until she pivoted and stumbled against him.

"I didn't want you to catch a chill," he said softly,

looking down at her parted lips, as she put a hand on his chest to catch her balance.

"Umm." She blinked up at him, then seemed to shake herself into awareness. "That was very thoughtful of you."

"Not that I'd mind your arms around me, your—"

"We really should be going!" She scooted around him, her purse banging him in the stomach—accidentally, he hoped.

As Case watched her walk briskly toward the sedan, he smiled into the cozy darkness surrounding Mandy's front porch. Next time, he'd bring the Harley. No matter what she said about practicality, she obviously wanted the wildness of wind stinging her cheeks, her legs wrapped around a powerful machine.

He was just the man to oblige.

She stopped and turned around, her purse clutched close to her side. Her imperious tone was probably effective in her library, but he found her adorable, not bossy. "Are you coming?"

His grin widened. "Your wish is my command."

CHAPTER SIX

Mandy patted her lips with the napkin and leaned back in her chair. "I may never eat again," she announced.

Case sat across the table, his own plate nearly empty. He stabbed the last piece of pickled green tomato and placed his fork beside his plate. "Me, too."

The waitress came by, asked if they wanted anything else, and then cleared off some of the dishes. Mandy wondered what she and Case would talk about now. He'd been such a perfect gentleman this evening that she was beginning to feel uncomfortable.

The idea that Case was being too good made her smile.

"What's up?" he asked, leaning forward and sipping his iced tea.

"I was just thinking, you've been such a perfect date that I'm wondering if some alien spacecraft came down and replaced the Case Gardner I know with a pod."

He laughed. "No, I'm just behaving myself, like I promised. Didn't you believe me?"

"Well, yes. But you said you wouldn't embarrass me in public. You didn't promise to be perfect."

His eyes twinkled with merriment. "I'm glad to know you think so highly of me, Mandy. I do aim to please."

"See, that's the old Case I know."

"Old Case? Watch it."

"I didn't mean to imply you're old."

"How old do you think I am?"

She suddenly felt uncomfortable. She hadn't meant to steer the conversation in this direction. "It's none of my business."

"Oh, come on. Surely you have an opinion."

"No, really."

He leaned closer. "Okay, I'll admit it. I'm forty-five."

"You are not!" She must have looked as shocked as she felt, because he started laughing. She frowned at him. "That's not fair."

"Sorry, but it's so easy to tease you."

She folded her arms and leaned back in her chair. "Okay, I give. How old are you?"

"I thought you'd never ask. I'm thirty-one."

"Really? That young!" She tried to use her most startled look and tone of voice.

"Now who's being incorrigible?" He tried to look stern, but she thought he failed miserably. There was just no way for Case to look anything but deliciously appealing.

"Would you like dessert?" he asked, leaning back as he casually asked the question.

Had he read her mind? Did he know she was thinking about him? Surely not . . . at least not that he'd make a scrumptious final course to their meal. "I couldn't eat another bite," she said before thinking how he might interpret her innocent comment.

His sexy grin made her realize he hadn't missed the sexual innuendo. "Sorry to hear that."

"Case, must you turn every comment into some sort of juvenile, hormone-heavy remark?"

"You said I was acting too perfect. I had to do something to redeem my image."

"In other words, you're damned if you do, damned if you don't."

"Well put, Miss Thompson."

"Thank you," she answered crisply, striving for her most professional voice. "I've really enjoyed the meal, but perhaps we'd better get back to Scottsville. I do have to get up early in the morning to go to church."

"And sing like an angel."

Mandy laughed. "Hardly. You've obviously never heard me sing."

"There are a lot of things I've never seen you do," he reminded her.

"You're welcome to visit me at church, of course."

"First my aunts, now you. Do I look as though I need redemption?"

As much as she wanted to remain professional and detached, she couldn't help teasing him. "At the moment or when you rode into town?"

He leaned forward again, his eyes focused only on her, his expression suddenly intense. "Which do you prefer?"

"That's really none of my business."

Case leaned back in his chair. "I'm beginning to wonder why you're avoiding any question that's the least bit personal."

"You're asking me to pass judgment on something."

"No, I'm not. I just want to know if you like the scruffy look or the clean-shaven one. Do you like the motorcycle more than the car?" He leaned closer, his eyes heavy-lidded and his voice intimate. "Do you like polite dinner conversation better than hot kisses in a dark library?"

The memory of those hot kisses came rushing back, along with the knowledge she'd again provoked Case into the dangerous, predatory male she half-feared and half-desired. "Don't," she whispered.

He looked at her so long that she shifted uncomfortably in her seat, breaking eye contact. "You're right. This isn't the place. And I did promise to behave myself in public." In one smooth motion, he pushed back his chair.

"I thought you agreed to behave yourself *on this date.*"

He pulled out her chair, leaned closer, and whispered in her ear, "No, just in public. And in just a minute, you're going to be alone with me in the car."

He straightened, giving her a sideways smile that made her heart race. After tossing several bills on the table, he folded his wallet and slid it back into his jeans pocket, where it immediately molded to the curve of his rear. She couldn't help but notice, since her eyes seemed to stray to that part of his anatomy with the least little encouragement.

Get your mind back on track, she tried to tell herself.

A couple of kisses, one date. Her attraction to him wasn't unusual, given the circumstances, and didn't make their relationship all that special.

Sure.

A gentle drizzle greeted them as they exited the restaurant. Lights placed high in the surrounding pine trees silvered the mist as they walked through the lot toward the car, giving the whole area a fairy-tale quality Mandy found quite appealing. It was even romantic.

Not that she was thinking of romance. Not that she should be thinking along those lines at all.

Like the gentleman he'd been for most of the evening, Case opened her car door. His hand skimmed along her hair as she started to get inside.

"You're sparkling with fairy mist," he said in a low voice.

She looked up towards the lights, which hid in the tall trees like shy, bright stars. "Strange, but I was just thinking that the night looked like something out of a fairy tale—so misty and quiet."

"Maybe there is magic out tonight."

"Maybe we just have active imaginations," she said softly.

His hand cupped her jaw, holding her captive as surely as a more forceful embrace. His gaze settled on her lips, which parted involuntarily. "Then can you imagine what I'm thinking right now?"

"Yes," she whispered.

He lowered his head, his lips as light as the misting rain, and brushed his mouth across hers. He tasted spicy and familiar; he felt warm and comforting on this cool night. This wasn't the kiss from the library, but rather a gentle, more reverent version Mandy found just as moving.

She blinked away the sudden moisture in her eyes. When she looked at his intense, arresting features, she saw a glow that came from within, not some artificial source. If she didn't know better, she would have given his look a name—one she had no business identifying, one she was afraid was reflected in her own expression. But he wasn't thinking of forever; he was here for only two months, and then he'd go back to the mystery life he led when not helping old ladies and flirting with shy librarians.

"We should leave," she said, breaking the spell.

"We should do a lot of things," he answered cryptically. He seemed to shake off the magic of the night as easily as water droplets from his dark, glistening hair.

Mandy eased into the passenger seat. Case closed her door, and she had only a moment to sigh before he settled into the driver's seat.

"I've decided to be on my best behavior while we're alone, too," he said as he started the engine. They both fastened their seat belts as he put the car in gear. "Just for tonight, I wanted to let you know."

"Well . . . thank you." She honestly didn't know what to say. Again, he'd surprised her.

"Just for tonight, though." He looked both ways, then pulled out onto the deserted state highway.

"Why?" she finally asked when the silence stretched between them as tight as a bowstring.

He glanced at her briefly before turning his attention back to the road. "Because you have to get up early in the morning and sing in the church choir. And if I don't behave myself tonight, you won't be getting up early—you'll be staying up until dawn. And your singing might sound a little hoarse to all those fine church members."

"Hoarse?" she said, her voice shaky.

"Mandy," he said, his knuckles white on the steering wheel, "when we have the time, I'm going to make you sing out in passion. I want you to be loud and joyous and totally unrestrained. I don't want you thinking about duties and obligations, or anything except *us*. So for tonight, I'm going to take you home, walk you to the door, and not come inside for even a minute."

He looked at her again, his eyes glowing from the red display of the dashboard, giving him a dangerous, almost unearthly appeal. "Do you agree?"

"Yes," she whispered, compelled to be honest with him despite her good intentions and her fears of once more losing control.

"Good," he said, rotating his hands on the steering wheel as though he was revving the engine on his Harley. "I'm glad we got that settled."

Case accompanied Millicent to church on Sunday, acting the part of the good nephew. His aunt looked proud as she walked down the aisle to her regular pew, her hand on his arm. He smiled and greeted all her friends, but when he looked toward the pulpit, he focused only on Mandy.

Dressed in a deep red robe with a scalloped white collar, she looked as prim and proper as ever. Only the blush on her cheeks when she spotted him showed the warm, expressive woman that hid beneath the traditional, conservative exterior.

Had he really spoken so frankly to her last night, announcing his intention to take her to bed, to make her cry out in passion? Yes, he thought with a smile as the minister began speaking. He certainly had been that blunt. She'd known what he meant—with a little clarification—and she hadn't bolted from the car or slapped his face.

He was gaining ground.

Mandy, he knew, would have thought about what he'd promised for most of last night, long after he'd left her with a chaste kiss to her cheek and a reminder to lock her door. She was probably thinking about their relationship right now, even as she opened her hymnal to begin the first song. Just to make sure, he sent her an intimate look meant for her alone. She buried her nose in the book.

"Case, the hymnal," Millicent reminded him.

"Yes, Aunt Millie." He took the well-worn book from the holder, releasing the smell of paper and leather that he'd associated most of his life with church—and libraries. The smell was the same in both places; the reverence he experienced had always calmed his soul.

"Mandy Thompson is looking at you," she whispered as the first notes of the organ rang out.

"Really? Then I suppose your matchmaking is working."

"What?" she blustered. She swatted his forearm gently as he held the hymnal between them. "I don't know what you're talking about."

"Shh, Aunt Millie," he said, smiling as he began to sing.

* * *

Mandy couldn't believe the boxes of books that arrived just after lunch on Monday. They were addressed to "Miss Mandy Thompson" at the temporary library's address, but contained no cover letter to let her know which person at the major New York publisher had authorized the shipment. Whoever had taken pity on the small town library, she sincerely wanted to thank them. Apparently the letters, sent by her and the Friends of the Library, had finally reached the right desk.

Wait until the library patrons saw these bestsellers! Her fingers itched to affix a book return pocket into each one and stamp "Scottsville Public Library" inside the front and back covers.

Her heart swelled with pride. She wanted to tell someone about the good fortune.

She wanted to tell Case, she realized suddenly, her hands pausing from unpacking her treasures.

Mandy took a steadying breath, knowing that she had more than a case of lust for a sexy bad boy. She'd begun to think of him as a friend, too, and that was more dangerous than considering him for a weekend fling. She'd kept herself busy working in the community and making new acquaintances in Scottsville, but she hadn't made any close friends, and she just now realized how lonely she'd become.

Case not only stimulated her hormones, he also provoked her mind. He challenged her to be honest about her emotions, something only a friend—or a lover—would do. He seemed to sense things about her she'd tried very hard to keep private, things she desperately wanted to share with someone.

"What am I going to do?" she said out loud, thankful for once that no one was in the library on this blustery afternoon.

She glanced at her watch. Ten minutes until two. Case would be closing the bakery in just a short while, and she had no idea what he would do then. He disappeared for hours each day, as far as she could tell, but then showed up unexpectedly. Where he went, she had no idea. She had never seriously considered asking, even though the question now seemed to burn a hole in her fragile self-control.

"Get a grip," she mumbled, moving a box of books out of the aisle. She was too excited to stay put; she'd worked hard all day, and she needed a little something to tide her over until dinner.

A cup of coffee. A cinnamon roll, perhaps. Maybe a few minutes of conversation with Case.

Just to share her good news.

With that image firmly entrenched in her brain, she pushed herself off the floor, dusted off her muted plaid skirt, and grabbed her purse and coat. The books could wait for their official library insignia, but she needed to see Case right now.

Case had seen the familiar brown delivery truck drive through the town square toward the temporary library, and he hoped that meant Mandy was getting a surprise—a good surprise. He knew she wanted to make this library a success, but he still didn't understand why she cared so much for a community where she had no family ties. From what he'd learned around the bakery, she'd simply applied for the job when the old librarian had retired. She'd moved here from Dallas, virtually starting over in unfamiliar territory, working with a limited budget and a well-meaning but inexperienced group of patrons. Then the library had burned down, and she'd faced rebuilding it with even less than had been available before.

Why? He wanted her to trust him enough to tell him. Maybe enticing her with sexual promises hadn't been the way, but he wanted to be honest with Mandy.

Well, about most things. At some point in their relationship, he'd have to explain that he wasn't an itinerant baker or mountain man or biker.

The clock on the wall chimed two. Millicent set it a few minutes early to remind herself when to lock up for the day. He'd taken over that task, though, so she could better take care of Greta after the morning rush at the bakery. He didn't mind being alone in the place; the quiet suited him, and the yeasty aromas stimulated his senses.

And speaking of stimulating, Miss Mandy was making her way toward the bakery as fast as her sensible leather shoes would carry her.

He dusted off his clothes and hands, then walked behind the counter and tried to look surprised when she arrived. Outside the glass door, she paused a moment to smooth back her windblown hair and compose her features. Then she tugged open the door, letting in a blast of cool, damp air.

"What a surprise," he said as he leaned across the counter, watching excitement sparkle in her dark eyes. "What brings you over on such a windy day?"

"I thought a cup of coffee and a roll sounded

good," she said, obviously trying to control her voice. "And I had some good news I wanted to share."

"With me?" Case tried to sound surprised as he reached for the coffeepot and poured them each a cup. "I'm really glad you came by. Let me lock up for the day, then we can sit down and talk."

She glanced at the door as if he'd suggested they go to the nearest motel and rent a room for an hour. Not a bad idea, but she really looked like she wanted to talk. "I don't want to keep you."

"Don't worry. My schedule is flexible." He jangled the keys on the way to the front door, making her eyes widen a little more. He chuckled at her involuntary reaction. "Don't worry, Mandy. I'll keep the shades open and the lights on, if you'll feel more secure that way."

She drew herself up. "No, I'm fine. Really. I just didn't want to inconvenience you."

He turned the key, then walked deliberately to where she stood near the front counter. With a smile, he reached down and touched her chin. "Haven't you figured out that it would be damned near impossible for you to inconvenience me? I'm a really understanding guy, Mandy. And patient."

He leaned down and kissed her cheek. "And I'd love to have a cup of coffee with you and hear your good news."

Flustered, her breath fast, she blinked at him with big, round eyes before taking a seat at the closest table.

Case smiled as he selected two cinnamon rolls from the display case, placed them on a tray with the coffee mugs, and carried it all to the table. "You take cream, don't you?" he asked, passing her the dainty china pitcher.

She fixed her coffee, appearing very much the prim and proper small town librarian. Case couldn't keep the smile off his face as he watched her. She fascinated him—the mystery, the hidden passion, the layers he wanted to peel away until he knew all her secrets.

And that meant telling her all of his.

"I just received a shipment of books from one of the big New York publishers," she said as soon as she folded her hands in her lap. "New, hardback bestsellers, plus some great classics. Some of the new releases aren't even in the bookstores yet!"

"That's great. Why do you think they sent the books?" he asked innocently.

"I . . . we did write many letters to the publishers, asking for donations. I hadn't heard from any of them, and then all of a sudden, I got this very generous shipment."

"I suppose someone up there got the message." He took a sip of coffee and watched her animated features over the rim.

"Yes, I believe that's what happened." Mandy picked up her cinnamon roll, then paused before taking a bite. "We even received several copies of Casey Flannigan's last mystery. I've been wanting to read that one ever since I saw the review in *Library Journal.*"

"Really? So you like mysteries," he said noncommittally.

"Yes, among other things. I'm not real fond of science fiction or horror, but I read almost everything else."

"So," he said, leaning back in his chair and balancing his coffee mug, "did you read the other Flannigan novels?"

"Yes. I like them very much. He seems to have such a grasp of his female characters, unlike some writers, who don't have a clue how to write anything but bimbos or man-haters."

Case chuckled, nearly sloshing coffee on his white T-shirt.

"Don't you agree? Or haven't you read his books?"

"Oh, I've read them. I'm just kind of surprised you assumed the writer was a he. I mean, Casey could be either a man's or a woman's name."

Mandy frowned. "You're right. I just assumed . . . I suppose I'm as guilty of sexism as everyone else."

"Don't look so disappointed. I'm sure something else about the writing made you think this Flannigan person is a man."

"No," Mandy said, her mouth pursed in contemplation, "I think you're right. Casey Flannigan may very well be a woman. The reviewers have never given any indication, so why not?"

Why not, indeed? Case smiled. "I'm glad you received the books. That's a nice surprise."

"Yes, it is. I just wish I knew who sent them so I could write a personal thank-you note."

"I'm sure the marketing director knows which individual arranged the shipment. Maybe you could just address the note to them."

"You're right," she said, then took a small bite of her roll. She frowned slightly. "You seem to know a lot about the publishing business."

"I have some friends in New York," he answered, finishing his coffee in one swallow. "So, do you need any help getting the books ready for the shelves?"

"No, but thanks. I'll get them classified and pre-pared tomorrow."

"Maybe you could let people know about the new books in the newspaper. Maybe even put up some flyers at local businesses."

"That's a good idea, but I don't have a computer at the library."

"I could get a flyer prepared for you," he offered carefully.

"Really?" She tilted her head to one side. "How?"

Case leaned forward, resting his forearms on the table, and smiled the way that made Mandy react like a woman, not a librarian researching a misfiled reference book. "Mandy, you ask too many questions, you know that? Just say, 'Yes, thank you, Case. That would be nice.' "

"I didn't mean to sound ungrateful."

"You didn't. I'm teasing you." He captured her hands before she could get all prissy and pull away. "Why don't we celebrate your good fortune? Greta and Millicent made some dandelion wine this spring, and they've just informed me it's ready for tasting. I know they'd love for us to have the first glass."

"I don't know . . . I've never tasted dandelion wine."

"It's an old family recipe. Very traditional. You don't want to hurt their feelings, do you?"

"Well, no, but I don't see how not tasting—"

"Then what time should I come by?"

"Um—how about seven o'clock?" she said, surpris-ing him . . . and herself.

CHAPTER SEVEN

Mandy got ready too early that evening. It was so early she had more than enough time to wonder what she was doing, having Case over to her house to drink wine. Would her neighbors notice his motorcycle parked out front? Had she chosen the right outfit for an evening at home?

"Oh, Lord," she whispered as she paced the length of her hallway. Part of her—the sensible side—wanted to calm down, put a bowl of peanuts on the coffee table, and wait patiently for Case to show up. The other part—the wild and crazy side—wanted to wear something more seductive than a blue sweat suit decorated with red bandanas and cheerful sunflowers. She'd bought the outfit at a local crafts fair, but the homey design didn't seem right for a night alone with a man like Case.

Of course, *she* wasn't right for a night alone with Case, either.

When she heard the rumble of his Harley, her first instinct was to bolt for the safety of her bedroom. She stood frozen to the floor. When the doorbell rang, the wild woman inside made her rush to the door and open it wide.

A cold wind blew in, bringing Case right along. Under one arm he held a paper bag wrapped around what must be the dandelion wine. The other hand held a small bouquet of bright yellow and dark maroon chrysanthemums.

"These are from my aunts' garden, but I swear I got their approval before I picked them," he said with a twinkle in his eyes.

"I believe you," she said, accepting the bouquet. How long had it been since she'd received flowers? Especially a hand-picked selection? Her eyes misted as she brought the blooms to her nose. "Thank you. Let me put these in water."

She hurried into the kitchen, but heard his boots on the hardwood floor as he followed at a more sedate pace. Case seemed to do everything in a deliberate, measured way. She wondered if he made love like that—slow and steady and powerful.

"Stop it," she muttered beneath her breath. She had no business thinking that way. He'd promised not to do anything she didn't want him to, but if he could read her mind, he'd be seducing her before the first glass of wine was consumed. And Case *did* seem to have an extraordinary ability to tell what she was thinking.

She grabbed an etched glass vase and turned on the faucet. When she turned around, he was stripping off his leather jacket, hanging it over the back of a kitchen chair.

"It's getting cold. I think the front they predicted for the early morning hours is coming through early," he said.

He wore a natural cotton fisherman's sweater over worn jeans that molded to his body in all the right places. His hair was windblown, his cheeks slightly pink from riding in the cold. She had the urge to hug him close, warm him up, and slide her hands underneath that bulky sweater.

She realized he was leaning against the table, letting her look her fill. And she'd certainly done just that. Embarrassed to be caught ogling, she broke eye contact and placed the flowers in the vase. "Do we need a corkscrew to open the wine?" she asked.

"No. They use the screw-on tops for the bottles. They make this stuff in a big crockery jar on the back porch. I had no idea Scottsville grew so many dandelion plants."

"They're welcome to the ones in my yard," Mandy said, reaching into her cabinet for some wineglasses. "I sure had a bunch this spring when I moved into the house."

"You really haven't been in Scottsville long, have you?"

"Less than a year. I had an apartment at first, then I found this house."

"It's perfect for you."

"Thank you." She wondered what he really meant by that comment, but was reluctant to ask. He'd tell her, and then she'd be faced with more of his insights that made her nervous.

Or excited.

She took a deep breath, then handed him the glasses. "Would you do the honor of pouring?"

"Of course." He made a great show of unscrewing the cap, then sniffing it. Mandy laughed at his theatrics. "Should we let it breathe?"

"I think it's breathed enough in that big crockery jar."

He poured a little, swished it around like the finest wine connoisseur, then took a sip. "Ah, yes. Definitely a 1998 Gardner vintage."

Mandy laughed. "Would you like something to eat? Or should I say cleanse your palate?"

"No, I'm fine. I had a big dinner with my aunts. Pot roast and potatoes. Between their cooking and the bakery, I'm going to weigh three hundred pounds by the time I roll out of town."

"Oh, I doubt that," Mandy said, glancing again at his wide shoulders, narrow hips, and long, muscular legs.

She accepted the wineglass he offered, feeling a bit warm. Perhaps she had set the furnace too high. Or maybe this sweat suit was too heavy for indoors.

"To your good fortune," he said, clinking his glass against hers.

She'd almost forgotten the reason for their meeting tonight. *Not a date,* she reminded herself. "Yes, to the library's good fortune."

"One and the same," Case said, taking a swallow.

She sipped, surprised at the sweetness of the wine. The flavor was different than one made with grapes, but just as fragrant. "This is good," she said, holding the glass up to the light. "I'm surprised."

"I'm not. I remember the taste from sampling one of their batches when I was only eleven. My aunts thought I'd fallen out of a tree and hit my head until they realized I was soused."

Mandy chuckled at the image, then put her hand over her mouth. "I shouldn't laugh about a child drinking alcohol."

"I wouldn't be so lenient with a child of my own, I suppose, but it was kind of funny when it happened to me. After my aunts discovered I'd raided their brew, they locked up the crock."

"Probably a good idea." She took another sip, then wondered if the adult Case Gardner should be under lock and key—just to save the women of the world from getting intoxicated on his good looks and sense of humor.

"Would you like to sit down in the living room?" she asked as soon as the idea popped into her head.

You just want to get him alone on the couch, the wicked voice inside her head advised.

"Sure." He put his hand around the stem of his wineglass. "Let me refill first."

He poured, seemingly oblivious to her rapid heart rate and quickened breath. When he'd topped off both of their glasses, he smiled. "After you."

She walked down the short hallway, well aware that he was behind her, watching. She tried to walk sensibly, but her hips wanted to sway seductively. Her back wanted to arch. She wanted to toss her hair and smile over her shoulder.

She didn't do any such thing, of course. She was going to have a hard enough time keeping him on his end of the couch.

"Do you have any music?" he asked when she paused near the sofa. He stood in the middle of the room, the bottle of wine still dangling from his long, strong fingers.

Stop thinking about him that way, she reminded herself. "Sure. What do you like?"

"Lots of things. Classic rock, good jazz, even a little country and western. Anything but hip-hop, punk rock, or rap."

"Darn," she said, walking to the CD player on her shelves, "and I just got 'Rapping to the Oldies' in the mail."

He chuckled. "I'd better pick," Case said, standing so close she could smell his tangy, woodsy aftershave. She had a strong urge to run her hand up his arm and around his neck.

"Go ahead," she said, hiding her attack of lust behind a ladylike sip of the sweet wine. "If you can master baking in those big ovens, I'm sure you can figure out how to operate the CD player."

"I'm good with my hands," he said with a grin.

Mandy smiled weakly and headed for the far end of the couch. How was she going to talk to him when all she could think about was how he would feel and taste? How good he smelled? How well he kissed?

She settled down as the music from *The Age of Innocence* wafted through the room. She'd almost forgotten she owned the soundtrack. The choice seemed an unlikely one for a motorcycle riding, passing-through-town guy like Case, but then, she'd often underestimated him. Sometimes she thought he misrepresented himself on purpose, but for what reason, she had no idea.

Maybe she'd just made too many assumptions based on stereotypes. Maybe she didn't know him at all.

He certainly didn't know her. Not the "her" she'd been before moving to Scottsville.

"Tell me why those books are so important to you,"

Case urged as he settled in beside her. "I know you're trying to rebuild the library, but I sense that this is more than just a job to you."

She watched the light play off the wine in her glass for several long moments before answering. "When I was a little girl, one of my favorite places was the public library. I loved the smell, the quiet. I spent hours roaming the stacks, reading at the tables."

The music swelled and ebbed, then he said, "The library sounds like it was a refuge for you."

Her breath caught in her throat. "How did you know?"

"Because," he said, tucking a lock of hair behind her ear, "it was the same for me."

She turned to look into his mysterious green eyes. The gold flecks seemed to glow with warmth on this cold evening, heating her blood. "You were lonely?"

He continued to stroke her hair. "Yes, back then. As I got older, I learned there was a difference between being alone and being lonely."

"So you're not lonely anymore?"

"Not, not usually, although sometimes when the snows come and the roads are blocked, and I get the urge to socialize, I feel isolated. Still, I know that the snow will melt, sooner or later, and I'll be able to get out and see my friends. Or meet new people."

Mandy saw the serenity in his eyes and knew he'd found peace of mind—a peace she'd never been able to achieve. No matter where she'd lived, she'd always felt isolated. This man, who lived in the mountains and was free to come and go, didn't feel as alone as she did in the midst of a welcoming community.

"Mandy, what's wrong?" Case touched the corner

of her eye gently. She'd shed a tear without being aware that her emotions were so close to the surface.

"I'm sorry. I just realized something . . . and I felt sad."

"Tell me."

"I envy the way you feel. The way you feel comfortable with yourself. I . . . I've never learned how to feel that way."

"Have you tried?"

"I think so." She frowned, wondering what he meant, wondering if she knew the answer to that simple question. To stall for time, she took a sip of wine.

"I probably have a few years on you. Maybe that's the difference," he offered.

"You're just saying that to be nice. I'm twenty-nine years old. I feel like I should have figured this stuff out by now." The wine was good, so she took another sip. Besides, she really was warm. She should go check the thermostat, but couldn't seem to work up the initiative right now, especially not with Case so close beside her. Why had she ever thought he should stay on his own end of the couch?

"I've had an advantage a lot of people don't," he said, rubbing her tense neck. "I've taken the time to get connected with who I am. While some people spend all their time at the office, or building their career, I took a different path."

"One that led you to a cabin in the mountains," she said, closing her eyes and leaning back into his massage.

"Among other places. The point is, I took time to discover who I am and what I want out of life. Maybe you haven't taken the time."

"Maybe not. But I've always known what I *should* be."

He turned her head toward his. She opened her eyes to see his serious expression. "You should be Mandy, that's all," he said in a low, intense voice. "Trying to be what someone else wants you to be is pointless." He paused, his eyes seeing far into the past. "No, it's worse than pointless. It's destructive. Living up to someone else's expectation will destroy who you are, bit by bit, until you can't find yourself anymore."

"Did you disappoint someone?" she whispered.

"Yeah, I did. My father wanted me to go into the military like him. Let's just say I wasn't an ideal candidate for routine and discipline. But that was a long time ago. I was younger then."

"But his disapproval hurt, didn't it?"

"Not as much as always feeling like a failure. As soon as I realized I wasn't going to be the son my father wanted, I felt liberated. Those goals were his, not mine. The fact that he couldn't accept me as I was became his problem, not mine."

"But what about society? What if it's more than just one person?"

Case shrugged. "Depends on which rules of society you're breaking."

He rubbed the cords on either side of her spine; the sensation was wonderful. She never wanted to get up off this couch. She never wanted to stop talking to him.

"You're not a murderer, are you?" he asked in a low, almost seductive voice.

"No, of course not!"

"Rob banks for a living?"

"No."

"Swindle old ladies out of their fortunes?"

"No! Don't be ridiculous."

"Then what expectations of society are you not living up to?"

She rolled her neck, the tension building back up. "You really don't want to hear this, do you?"

"Yes. I really do." Case leaned forward, refilling her wineglass. She hadn't realized it was empty. "Just relax and talk to me."

"I think I might be more relaxed if I didn't tell you."

"Chicken," he teased, a challenging glint in his eyes.

"Absolutely."

"Then use the false courage," he said, nodding toward her wineglass.

"That's a bad habit."

"Socially unacceptable," he added.

"Yes. Unhealthy."

"Maybe. But do you sit around and drink dandelion wine often?"

"No, this is a first."

"Then you don't have a bad habit. Think of this as a therapy session. I'll pretend to be your psychoanalyst."

Mandy smiled, feeling the effect of the wine. "You mean you want to play doctor?"

Case groaned. "Don't even suggest playing around unless you're serious."

"You're right. I shouldn't tease you."

"You can tease me all you want, but only if you're going to follow through—sooner or later."

"Hmm, that's rather vague. Maybe later." She

pushed up from the back of the couch, but had a little trouble getting her feet under her.

"Let me help," Case offered, standing up with ease and holding out his hands.

"I can get up. I just . . . I've been sitting too long."

"Um-hmm," he murmured, smiling down at her in a knowing way.

"I can hold my liquor," she said. "Besides, this is just wine, and I only had one glass." She put her hands in his and let him pull her to her feet.

"Two," he corrected. "Do you need any more help?" He looked so darn sure of himself, standing there in her living room, so confident and sexy.

She stood a little straighter and pulled down the hem of her knit top. "No. I'm just going to put on a new CD and get us some snacks." Food would be good to counteract the effect of the alcohol, and she had to check on the thermostat. This room was nearly steamy with heat. She had to be wasting money on her gas bill.

"Okay. I'll stay right here."

Promise, she thought as she walked carefully away from the coffee table toward the shelving unit. *Promise you won't leave. Promise you aren't some figment of my imagination.*

She smiled back at him as she ejected the CD. Darn, he was one nice, good-looking man—and that wasn't just the dandelion wine speaking.

Case knew he should be a gentleman and put the bottle of wine away, but Mandy seemed to enjoy it. For once, she was talking and asking questions. He liked that. He liked her interest a lot. Without a shred of conscience, he refilled her glass.

Right now, she was fumbling around in the kitchen. He should probably go in there and help her, but she looked as though she needed a few minutes alone. He didn't want to frighten her, and coming up behind her would no doubt make her jump.

Case spread his arms across the back of the couch and leaned his head against the thick pillows. He didn't mind talking about his past; the pain had long ago settled into a dull ache in the farthest region of his heart. If his revelations helped Mandy, then he'd reveal his life's lessons all night.

She quickly returned, carrying a small assortment of cheese and fruit. The slices had been artfully arranged on a blue and white plate, but the offering held little appeal. The hostess, on the other hand, looked pretty darn delicious.

"I like that outfit, by the way. I forgot to tell you earlier. It's very cheerful."

"Thank you," she said, placing the food on the coffee table. "But I think it's a little too warm. I'm going to check the thermostat."

"Fine with me," he said with a grin. He knew just how she felt. The heavy sweater had felt good beneath his jacket on the ride over here, but was a bit toasty for snuggling on the couch with Mandy.

While she checked on the heating system, he walked across the room and flipped off the brightest of the three lamps. Much better. He settled back on the couch.

She returned in just a moment, a nervous smile on her face. He'd have to work double hard to get her relaxed again, now that she'd had time to think about how good he'd made her feel. Her aversion to pleasure was one of the areas where he'd made some progress.

"We were just about to play doctor," he said, patting the seat next to him.

"I don't think *we* agreed to that." She sat on the end and focused on the plate of cheese and fruit, finally spearing a chunk of pineapple with a colored toothpick.

"We were going to talk about those societal expectations you aren't living up to."

"I . . . You really don't want to hear about that," she hedged. "I was just—"

"Speaking from the heart," he finished for her before she could back off again. "Now stop acting like a nineteenth-century virgin and come here."

He put an arm around her shoulders and dragged her against his side. She let out a small squeal, but gave only token resistance. He had a suspicion she liked the domineering act every now and then.

With his other arm, he reached for her wine. "The doctor says you need to take a little more medicinal spirits."

"The doctor is a bully," she said as she accepted the glass.

"If you're going to be difficult, I'll need to get more forceful."

Her wide, dark eyes flew open, surprise lighting her features. "What are you talking about? I'm not going to let you—"

"Yep," he said, exaggerating a drawl. "If you don't follow the doctor's orders, I'm going to have to tickle you."

"Tickle?"

He raised an eyebrow. "You are ticklish, aren't you, Miss Mandy?"

Surprise turned to wariness, then excitement. "Don't you dare."

"Only if I'm forced to," he warned. "Now take a sip, relax beside me, and tell me all your deep, dark secrets."

She opened her mouth to speak, then glanced around the room. "Is it dark in here?"

"No, it's just right. Now sip, then talk."

To his surprise, she complied. He suspected she was enjoying herself. He certainly was.

"I don't think I'm a bad person," she said in just a moment. "And I only have one deep, dark secret."

"You can trust me not to tell."

Mandy giggled. Case's heart swelled at the sound, so unfamiliar yet delightful. He wondered how often she let herself relax enough to laugh out loud.

"I . . . I kind of have to show you."

Show him? Now that sounded interesting, unless discovery involved getting up off this couch.

She grinned shyly at him. "I feel silly."

"You can do or say anything around me, Mandy," he reassured her, hoping that was indeed the case.

"Okay, well, here goes." She reached for the waist of her pants, and before he knew what she planned, he was staring at the upper portion of her pale, creamy bottom.

With a perfectly executed tattoo staring back at him.

CHAPTER EIGHT

Mandy lay on the couch as Case stared at her tattoo. At least he seemed to be focusing on the art and not the canvas, so to speak.

He leaned closer. "What is it?"

"A bookworm. That was my nickname in school." She twisted, trying to see the small tattoo, high on her right buttock. "He's inside a book, see? And he's wearing glasses."

"Oh." Case leaned even closer.

The reality of him braced above her, concentrating so completely on that particular part of her body, made her head swim. His shoulders blocked out much of the light, making her think of situations far more intimate than viewing a silly tattoo.

He looked up and grinned. "Mandy, you've really shocked me. I knew you had a few surprises, but never this. Who would have thought that the prim and

proper Miss Mandy Thompson had a bookworm tat-
tooed on her butt?"

"No one in Scottsville, that's for sure."

"I take it you've had this a while."

"Since my sophomore year in college."

"You just got an urge to get a tattoo?"

"A group of us went out one night, one thing led
to another, and we all ended up in a tattoo parlor—
a very nice one, I should add—and got our nicknames
or favorite characters permanently inscribed."

"In other words, you and some girlfriends got
drunk and went a little crazy."

She laughed, then put her hand over her mouth.
"I shouldn't have showed you."

"Oh, yes you should have." The gleam in his eyes
changed from teasing to intimate. "And I think I
need a closer look."

"No, wait."

He ignored her, of course, dipping his head until
she felt his hot breath on her skin, and, suddenly,
the brush of his lips on the silly design.

When he changed from a caress to a kiss, she practically melted into the soft cushions.

"Oh, Case," she whispered when she felt his hand
skim up her back and his weight settle against her
legs.

She closed her eyes against the swirling lights and
powerful sensations, reaching for him as he kissed
his way from her buttock to her waist. She knew she
should stop this madness, but didn't have the will-
power to say no. She'd been so good, so long. Her
body pressed close to satisfy needs long ignored, but
her heart craved more.

More than Case might be willing to give. Perhaps more than she was ready to admit.

With a twist, he pulled her beneath him, and framed her face with his warm hands. Her eyes opened, and she gazed up at his fierce, raw expression as he settled between her thighs.

He took her breath away.

"You're not just doing this to prove you can be bad, are you?"

"What?" She felt as though she had cobwebs in her brain. "What do you mean?" All she wanted to feel was his arousal pressed tight against her. She wondered if he knew how much she wanted to feel his skin against hers.

"You were a lot wilder when you were younger, weren't you? That's why you're trying so hard to be good now."

"Don't be a psychoanalyst, Case. Just kiss me. Forget the tattoo. Forget everything."

"Maybe I don't want to forget," he said softly. Suddenly he kissed her with a passion she hadn't experienced before. She felt possessed, both by his strong, hot body and by the fierceness of his kiss. His weight pressed her into the soft cushions until she felt both safe and reckless. If only they could stay this way forever, ignoring the world outside.

How odd that she felt this way. She tried so hard to be the best, the ideal. What power did Case have that he could make her change so much in only one night? And why did he want to know about her past, or understand her in the present, when he was only passing through?

"Mandy," he whispered against her lips, "we're not ready for this."

"We're not?" She pressed tighter against him.

"No. And I'm not going to take advantage of you when you've been drinking."

"I haven't had that much to drink."

"Yes, you have. That wine is potent stuff, stronger than you're used to, I'd bet."

"But I've wanted this. I really have. I just wouldn't admit it."

"Ah, Mandy, I know that. But what about in the morning? Are you ready to wake up with me beside you and not regret what we did? Are you ready to tell Scottsville that you've spent the night with the Gardners' nephew, who's just in town for a couple of months?"

She stared into his eyes, knowing she wasn't ready for either of those events, and hating herself for not having the courage to admit their relationship to the world.

"You're right," she said, turning away. "I'm a coward."

He urged her to look at him again. "No, you're not. You've very carefully constructed a life for yourself here in this town. I'd like to understand why, though. Just because you got a tattoo in college, and went out on the town once in a while, doesn't make you a bad person."

"Oh, I know I wasn't *bad*. But it was more than just having a good time. I couldn't focus on my courses. Any time someone came up with a fun thing to do, I was all for it. I changed my major three times— basically, whenever I discovered a topic I thought sounded more interesting."

"So you didn't know what you wanted to do right away. Lots of college kids don't."

"I nearly flunked out of school in my junior year because I didn't go to class. I never studied. I almost lost my grant money, and I was faced with paying back student loans when I didn't even have a degree."

"You got scared."

"Yes, I did, but that only made me behave for a short time. I managed to graduate with a degree in English Literature, but then I realized I didn't want to teach. I remembered my childhood, and how I felt about libraries, and I decided to get my master's degree in library science."

"So you continued in school, and you straightened up."

"Mostly. I had to work part time and take summers off. It took me longer than usual to get my degree. After I graduated, I got a job in the Dallas Public Library."

"That's good, isn't it?"

"Yes, and I began paying off my loans. I met new friends, I dated, and I slipped into the singles lifestyle that is so big in Dallas."

"You began to party again."

"Yes, and I took fun courses like scuba diving and cake decorating. I learned about ordering wine and painting watercolors. In short, I started drifting from one thing to another, just like in college."

"And this frightened you?"

"Not at first. I was having too good a time. Then I realized I was running short of money each month, and I was tired all the time, and my life was basically a wreck."

"You're being awfully hard on yourself."

"No, I'm not. I've never lived up to my potential." She'd heard those words so many times, first from her parents, and more recently, from herself. "I've been lazy and distracted most of my life, as my parents would certainly tell you. I could have done a lot if I'd stuck to one thing instead of flitting from one hobby to the next."

"But Mandy, you weren't hurting anyone. Why are you so hard on yourself for being what everyone else would say is normal?"

"Because I *was* hurting someone—myself. I should have been able to control myself, but there seemed to be something wrong with me that kept me from focusing. And before you ask, no, I don't have any type of learning disability. I'm just . . . irresponsible. I can't seem to get my life together."

He looked deeply into her eyes. "Hey, I don't really understand why you think you have to be perfect, but I want you to know that I think you're wonderful. And lovely. I could spend a lifetime learning everything about you. I can't remember ever having more fun than trying to get you interested in me."

She stared at him, wondering if she'd lost her hearing—or her mind. He thought getting *her* interested in *him* was fun? "You're just being kind. You've known from the first that I was interested. I could see it in your eyes."

"Ah, but I thought you might think I was the human equivalent of a new species of bug. I could tell I wasn't the kind of person you usually spent time with."

"That doesn't mean I . . . never mind." She'd almost admitted how much she'd wanted him from the first. "Maybe I have had too much dandelion wine."

"Then I should probably go, before my willpower gives out."

"Yes, I suppose that would be best," she said, trying to keep the disappointment out of her voice and failing miserably.

Case smiled. "Always doing the right thing."

"Not always. Tonight, you were the good one."

He leaned down and kissed her, briefly, sweetly. "That won't always be the case," he promised.

Then he pushed up from the cushions, and she felt the loss of his heat and weight as though he'd pulled away a part of herself.

Case roared out of town on his Harley, letting the cold wind and dampness do what his good intentions could not—cool his blood. He'd done the right thing in leaving Mandy, but that didn't mean he liked it.

Somewhere on State Highway 155, northeast of Scottsville, he realized what was really bothering him. More than the denial of passion, more than the frustration of looking at the longer term relationship, he felt like he'd let Mandy down because he'd told her so little about himself. Just a snippet about his past, his father.

He'd let on nothing about the man he was today.

"Dammit," he muttered, slowing the big machine as he came to an intersection. This charade of his had to stop. She needed to know who he was and why he could pull up stakes to help out his aunts at a moment's notice. Mandy thought he was unemployed, and he hadn't told her differently. He saw the questions in her eyes, but he hadn't bothered to answer them.

Maybe he wanted to believe she would want him anyway, even if she thought he was an itinerant biker who lived in a tiny cabin in rural Colorado. Tonight, she'd shown that she wanted him—at least physically—but she hadn't wanted to admit to the world that she lusted after his body.

Would she have told her friends and neighbors how she felt if he were a stockbroker or a lawyer? Would she still keep their relationship a secret?

Case paused beside the highway, letting the evening breeze whip through his hair and sting his chapped cheeks. Which was more important: the truth about his career or the truth about Mandy's feelings for him as a man?

Did he trust her enough to take the chance?

He eased open the throttle, shifting through the gears as he picked up speed. There was no reason to decide tonight. He needed to think about his options for a while. Tomorrow, Mandy would probably feel bad about what had happened between them tonight.

Despite his doubts, a smile creased his face as he remembered when she'd pulled down her waistband to show him the tattoo. He'd said he was surprised, but that didn't accurately express his shock. He'd forgotten to breathe for a second. He'd stared at her butt as if he'd never seen one before.

He'd recovered, of course. He'd found the small piece of body art sexy, especially when he'd imagined the wildness inside of her. And he couldn't help but kiss the spot.

Dry leaves skittered beneath the extended front forks of the Harley as he roared toward home. He'd think about Mandy's probable reaction to learning about his career, and figure out whether she wanted him, the unemployed biker, or someone else. Someone more acceptable.

There would be time to make a decision. There was no rush. He wasn't going anywhere for seven weeks, and he could wait another week or two to get Mandy into his bed, even if she was already in his heart.

He didn't want to think about leaving her, though. He wasn't ready for *that*. Not yet.

Mandy would have been late for work the next morning if she'd been able to go back to sleep after waking up at five o'clock. With her stomach queasy and her mouth feeling like she'd swallowed cotton balls, she'd stumbled into the kitchen and downed a big glass of orange juice. Only after the last swallow had she remembered the juice was acidic and probably not the best choice for a post-dandelion wine morning.

She spent the rest of the pre-dawn hours nursing an Alka-Seltzer and recalling each embarrassing moment of the last evening. Had she really pulled her pants down and shown Case her tattoo?

"Of course you did, you ninny," she mumbled to herself as she eyed the dregs of the fizzling drink.

The sun broke the horizon as she pulled her car out of the driveway. She would have walked, but pounding the pavement, even in her sensible shoes, was more than she could tolerate. If she got to work early, she could get the books classified and out on the shelves before anyone came to the library.

She could also avoid going by the bakery.

She wasn't ready to see Case. If he looked at her

in that knowing way of his, if he said anything at all, she might just die of embarrassment.

Telling him about her past wasn't the worst part of the evening. Heck, showing him the tattoo was stupid, but not that big a deal. No, the thing that made her really cringe was the way she'd practically begged him to make love to her.

Just like the small town prude she seemed to be, she'd gone after the hunk on the Harley like a woman desperate for a man. He must think she was pitiful. He probably never wanted to be alone with her again, no matter what he'd said.

Carefully, she unlocked the door to the temporary library. Dawn's rosy glow was reflected in the glass windows, creating a beautiful array of pinks, lavenders, and blues. If only she could enjoy the sight. If only she hadn't made a fool of herself last night.

With a groan, she rested her aching head against the cool glass. Who was she fooling? The *worst* part of last night had been her inexcusable rudeness when he'd asked her if she was ready to let the world know about their relationship. She'd insulted him, pure and simple.

She pushed open the door and slipped inside before someone on their way to work in Tyler or Longview saw her standing outside looking miserable and lost, which was exactly what she felt. She needed to be circumspect and conservative, she told herself, but rudeness was unacceptable in any circumstance, especially to a man who'd given her only compliments, offered to help sort books, and even volunteered to make some phone calls to get authors in for the Harvest Festival library fundraising.

She sat her purse on the makeshift checkout desk

and sank into a chair. When had she actually become so straight-laced, remaking herself to fit conservative small town notions of what was proper? Somewhere along the way, she'd adopted the dress and manners of a neurotic old maid who would rather insult a perfectly nice man than admit her feelings for him.

Somehow, she had to make things right. Publicly. She had to show Case she wasn't embarrassed to be seen with him. Not that she was going to throw herself at him again. Mandy shuddered. She'd never begged a man before, and this was a really bad time to start.

No, she needed to be around him in a friendly manner, which meant marching over to the bakery when it opened, apologizing for her behavior last night, and then showing the residents of Scottsville that she was friendly with Case Gardner.

Not romantic. She didn't need to admit something that personal. She wouldn't advertise the fact that she was attracted to any man. Her decision wasn't because he rode a Harley and would be gone before the new year. The sadness she felt at that reminder made her gloomy mood even worse. Not even the rising sun and clear skies improved her disposition. Only action would clear her mind and her conscience.

Poor guy. Coming to town to help his aunts, getting involved with a mixed-up librarian. He deserved better.

She grabbed her wallet and keys and glanced at her watch. Just past seven o'clock. The bakery was open by now. She had to push her reservations aside and show Case she wasn't embarrassed to be his friend.

She just hoped she could look at him in the light

of day without remembering how his lips had felt on her bare skin last night.

"Mandy! How nice to see you."

Millicent's high-pitched voice cut through the morning's silence like a hot knife through butter. Case stopped dropping teaspoonfuls of dough on a cookie sheet and turned around.

He hadn't expected her to show up. He thought she would be too embarrassed to see him this soon.

"Good morning," he said, dusting off his hands.

Her breath caught in her throat for a moment, then she smiled stiffly and said, "Hello, Case."

"You look like you need some coffee, Mandy," Millicent said.

Mandy winced. "I'm not sure. Maybe some herbal tea."

"Are you feeling poorly, dear?"

"Just a little." She put a hand on her stomach and smiled at his aunt. "I might have had a bit too much of your dandelion wine."

Millicent laughed. "That's easy to do. Greta and I just have a glass every now and then, for medicinal purposes, of course. I've been told it's stronger than the wine you buy in stores."

"I can believe that."

A mother and child came in. "I'll take care of Mandy, Aunt Millie," Case said cheerfully.

"Good!" His aunt bustled over to the display case. "Take your time."

Case waited until Mandy looked up, making eye contact again. She did look a little green around the gills, as his mother used to say. She also looked nervous, like she wanted to say something distasteful. If she started in on him about how he'd taken advantage of her last night, he wasn't sure how he would react. Sure, he'd given her wine, but that had only lowered her defenses. She'd simply revealed her true feelings. He had a feeling she was about to deny the truth they both knew.

He pushed the basket of tea bags across the counter. "Pick one."

"Can you take a break with me?"

"Sure." He poured boiling water into a mug and coffee for himself. For good measure, he grabbed two cinnamon rolls hot out of the oven.

Mandy helped him carry the items to a table in the back of the seating area of the bakery. He hid his surprise that she'd chosen such a private location. Of course, if she wanted to give him grief over his behavior, this spot would be better than where everyone could hear.

"I'm sorry you're not feeling well," he said as he took a seat. "Homemade wine is potent stuff. I should have warned you."

"It's my fault," Mandy admitted, unwrapping the tea bag. The smell of peppermint blended with cinnamon and sugar. "I shouldn't have had so much, especially since I'm not used to drinking anymore."

"And the rest of the night? Are you sorry about that, too?"

She dunked the tea bag and started to swish it around. Her blush brought color to the pallor of her cheeks. "Just one thing."

"Showing me the tattoo?" he whispered so no one else would hear.

"No." She jerked furiously on the bag, pumping

the aroma into the air around them. "I'm sorry I insulted you."

He frowned. "Insulted me? I don't remember——"

"When I admitted I wasn't ready to tell anyone you'd been to my house or that we'd gone on a date. That was rude, and I'm sorry."

"Mandy, I didn't think you were rude. I thought you were being practical. I assume you don't tell everyone about your personal life." He wanted to cover her hands with his, but knew the public show of affection wouldn't be welcome.

"Case, I didn't mean to insult you, but I did. I know you think I act too prim and proper most of the time," she said, dipping her head for a moment to hide behind her mug of tea. She straightened, meeting his gaze. "But I want you to know that your . . . well, your appearance and the fact that you're just passing through town, didn't have anything to do with my reaction last night."

He frowned as he leaned back in his chair. "So you're telling me that you weren't being a snob when you said you didn't want anyone to know I was at your house."

"I know it seems like I was snobbish, but that's why I wanted to come by. I wasn't thinking about you at all. I was just thinking about how others would see *me*."

"So what you're saying is that I could be a two-headed, bright pink alien from outer space, and that wouldn't have mattered, because your neighbors weren't expecting you to be alone with anyone."

"That's a rather strange and radical way to say it, but, yes, I suppose so."

"Okay, then on the other scale, if I were a pin-striped suited lawyer who drove a Mercedes instead of a Harley, you still wouldn't want to tell people you were alone with me."

"That's right. See, it's just *me.*"

"So you're not a snob."

"No, I don't think so."

"What if I were a lawyer here in town? Would that be different?"

"I . . . I don't know. I suppose it depends on how long we'd known each other."

"But that would be more acceptable?"

"Stability is important," she said, frowning. "I don't know what you're getting at."

"I'm getting at the fact that you think I'm some sort of bum." He knew he shouldn't get angry, but the more she apologized, the more he realized she'd done her best to stick him into a category—one that was safe for her. He didn't like being pigeonholed—with a nice, neat label underneath.

He especially didn't like to hear such nonsense from Mandy.

"I don't think you're a bum!"

"Why? Because I have a job at the bakery?"

"No, of course not. You're Greta and Millicent's nephew, for one thing. And you must have some income, or did in the past, because that motorcycle cost a fortune."

"I see," Case said, sounding more and more annoyed. "You've come to these conclusions on your own."

"Yes."

"You didn't ask anyone else about me, did you?"

She wouldn't have, of course, because to do so would show her interest.

"No."

"You never asked me, did you?"

"No . . ." She hesitated long enough to make him aware of how very hard she'd tried to keep their relationship impersonal—until last night. "I didn't want to be nosy."

"You didn't *want* to know much about me, did you?"

She dropped her gaze. At least she realized how hard she'd pushed him away. His persistence in seeking a relationship had only weakened her resolve enough to admit a physical attraction. She wanted nothing more from him than sex.

The silence stretched between them. In the background, he heard the old-fashioned register ring up a sale, then the door open and close. He couldn't stand this tension between them, but he'd be damned if he'd apologize for wanting more than a little of her affection.

"Dammit, Mandy, you should have asked."

She looked up, surprised that he was angry.

"Why are you angry? I was respecting your privacy."

"Maybe I wanted you to get nosy," he said, shifting his coffee cup out of the way. "Maybe you shouldn't have been so quick to make assumptions about me."

"Case, what—"

"I've got to get back to work," he said, pushing away from the table before he said something he'd regret later. He was just a hairbreadth away from creating a scene in his aunts' bakery and just a few seconds away from going way beyond socially acceptable behavior with the Scottsville librarian.

"I don't understand," she said as he walked away.

He didn't answer, because he wasn't sure how to explain something as complicated, and yet as simple, as his life.

CHAPTER NINE

Mandy spent the next two days letting everyone know about the new books, even passing out flyers she'd asked the printer to create. She'd taken the initiative herself, since Case had offered to make them up for her. He obviously wasn't going to help. Though he wasn't speaking to her, his suggestion was still a good one.

She just had to be more creative, she realized, in promoting the library. That meant asking for favors, even to the point of being a little pushy when merchants said they weren't sure where to place the flyers. She'd simply taken a roll of tape and stuck the lime green paper to the inside of their front window.

One of the nicest people she'd approached was Jillian Patterson, who owned the pet store. Jillian had a stepson in kindergarten, and she'd been very supportive of the library. She'd even volunteered her husband, Brad, to create future flyers and ads, and she'd promised she would speak to him about getting a computer for the library, either donated or at a discount. That wasn't as good as having an integrated system, but a computer would help her maintain records.

Mandy felt better after talking to the pet store owner and had even spent some time with the cute puppies she'd admired from the other side of the glass. Perhaps soon she would treat herself to a pet. At least some living creature would welcome her home each evening, she thought as she walked back to the library. Something nice and uncomplicated, whose needs could be met with food, water, walks, and pats on the head.

Unlike men, who wanted who-knew-what out of life.

By the time she walked back to the library, unlocked the door, and flipped on the lights, she was in a bad mood again. Darn Case, for making her spend even one second on unproductive thoughts. How was she supposed to get anything accomplished when she was fuming about his remarks? And who would have thought he'd want her to be nosy about his past? Or his present? From her experience, the fewer questions a woman asked a man about his personal life, the better he liked it.

What made Case Gardner so different?

"I don't want to think about him," she mumbled to herself. The red light on the answering machine was blinking, which gave her a good excuse to stop thinking about her personal problems and start concentrating on running the library. She hit the replay button a little harder than necessary.

"Miss Thompson, this is Valerie Boyd, publicist for

Casey Flannigan's publisher. I understand that you'd like to set up a fundraising book signing for your library. If you're interested, please call me back."

Mandy scrambled for a pen and paper, jotting down the New York phone number. First the books, then this phone call! What was happening all of a sudden? This was too good to be true!

She had to tell someone! Flipping open her address book, she looked for Mrs. Wilkins's number. Surely the Friends of the Library president and board would want to arrange a book signing by a well-known author. Mandy was just about to dial when she realized she needed more information. She'd better call the publicist first. And she'd better calm down!

After calculating the time in New York, she figured Ms. Boyd would still be at the office. She took a deep breath and dialed. Within seconds, she had the publicist on the line.

"Thank you for calling about a book signing. We'd love to have Casey Flannigan, especially if we could arrange it for our Harvest Festival on October 31. Do you think that's possible?"

She sighed in relief when she learned Casey Flannigan was available. "What about the books? Would we need to buy them from you or—"

"No, that's already been taken care of. The books will be a donation to your library."

"That's so generous! Especially on top of the box of books your company sent last week."

"You must have a guardian angel," Ms. Boyd said, humor evident in her voice. "I'll ship those out in the next two days."

"Thank you. Will we need to arrange for a hotel

for Casey Flannigan? And could you tell me if that's Mr. or Ms. Flannigan?''

"Oh, definitely mister,'' the woman said with a small chuckle. ''You'll know what I mean when you see him.''

"Really? I'm looking forward to it, then.'' Maybe he'd be as good looking as Case Gardner, which would do a lot to sell books.

Darn it, how could she think about him at a time like this? "And the hotel?''

"I believe he's making his own arrangements.''

"I'd be glad to give you or him a list of bed-and-breakfasts in town. And there's a motel nearby, although nothing right in Scottsville.''

"Please, don't worry. He said arrangements had already been made.''

One less thing for her to worry about, which was good. She was going to have to scramble to get the notices out about this big event and take people up on their offers to help. "Well, this is so wonderful. I'm looking forward to meeting him. I've read everything he's written since his first book, and I just started his latest.''

They chatted for just another minute, then Mandy said goodbye. She felt as though she was floating on air by the time she called Mrs. Wilkins.

Only as Mandy was closing up for the day did she pause to consider the conversation with the publicist. Something nagged at her mind. There was something about the arrangements . . .

Yes, now she recalled. Ms. Boyd had said that Casey Flannigan had already made arrangements for his accommodations. How could that be? Mandy had only just given her the date of the Harvest Festival on the phone.

How did Casey Flannigan make reservations before he knew when he was supposed to be in town?

And how had the publicist known she would love to have this one specific author for a book signing?

Case stopped the Harley across the street from the temporary library, watching Mandy check books out for two small kids. She smiled at them, but Case couldn't tell if she was just going through the motions or if she was really happy. Whenever he'd seen her around town, she'd worn a don't-bother-me expression. To publicize the new books and the library in general, she'd visited every business around the square—except the bakery.

Millicent had received her flyer through the mail.

He sighed, wondering if Mandy was ready to hear his explanation, his apology, for reacting so strongly to her at the restaurant the other morning. She'd been trying to explain how she thought she'd insulted him, and he'd turned the tables on her and gotten angry.

His anger had been justified, perhaps, because of the assumptions she'd made. But he was partially to blame for letting her believe he was a bum. How could he be so angry at Mandy for being true to herself? She was afraid of being as irresponsible as she had been apparently, before moving to Scottsville. She was afraid of getting involved with the wrong kind of man and of letting other people think of her as too wild for small town life.

If he had told her who he was up front, he wouldn't be sitting here in the cool, late afternoon, wondering how he was going to bridge the gap that had opened between them.

Case set the stand and swung his leg over the bike. He missed her, pure and simple. Now that he'd set his other plan in motion, he needed to "fess up," as his aunts would say.

The two children exited just as he stepped up to the door. He held the door open for them, slipping inside before Mandy knew he was there.

She stood at the checkout desk, her smile gone now that she thought she was alone. Dressed in a creamy cotton turtleneck and a blue plaid jumper, she looked as prim and proper as ever. Only the circles under her eyes and the listless expression on her face showed her true feelings.

He hoped he hadn't caused her any sleepless nights.

"Hello, Mandy."

She jumped, her gaze flying to his as she dropped the pen she'd been holding. Her lips parted in an "o," making him want to take advantage of her surprise and kiss her senseless.

"Case, I didn't hear you come in."

"I took the opportunity to slip in when the kids left."

"Then you've been spying on me."

"Guilty as charged," he said, stepping farther into the library. "But you weren't doing anything but doodling. I don't think I've uncovered any national security secrets." He looked down at the scribbled-up paper on her desk, but she quickly placed a book about a fuzzy caterpillar on top.

"Or maybe I did," he said, looking into her eyes. "Mandy, I'm sorry."

She took a deep breath and raised her chin. "I don't understand what happened the other morning."

"I know you don't. That's why I'm here."

"I . . ." She looked around the library as if someone was going to come to her rescue, but then garnered her courage and stood even straighter. "I was just getting ready to lock up for the night."

"Then if you don't have plans, why not go somewhere with me so we can talk? I'd love to buy you dinner."

She looked outside at his Harley and swept her hand down her jumper. "I'm not dressed for a ride on your motorcycle."

"Is that the only reason you can think of?"

"Are you asking me if I've changed my mind about telling people we've seen each other socially?"

"Mandy, I don't remember our dates being particularly social. I wasn't spending time with the town; I was spending it with you."

"Yes, I know. And I won't bore you with the assumption that I'm going to be the person left in town when you leave. I'll be the one answering questions about what you were like, what we possibly had in common—"

"Tell them the truth, or tell them nothing. Whatever happens between us is our business."

"That's pretty naive. You must know how small town gossip feeds on ignorance and supposition."

Case sighed. "Mandy, that's not what I wanted to

talk about. Please. I have something to tell you, and I don't particularly want an audience."

"Well, I have something to tell you, too. I'll go to dinner with you, in front of witnesses and everything. I'm not ashamed to be seen with you. I just don't want people talking about me all over Scottsville. This is where I plan to live; this is the library I'm going to rebuild."

He watched her across the space of the desk, aware that she'd been doing a lot of thinking in the past two days. He was going to give her something new to occupy her mind. "I hope you won't change your mind about going out with me after I tell you my secret."

"Your secret?"

"Yes. I should have told you the other night, but you were so darn cute confessing all of yours that I didn't have the time or the inclination."

She blushed all the way to her pretty pink ears, and he couldn't stop himself from teasing her just a little. "I saw the way you were looking for the Harley the other day when we went to dinner. Why don't you change into jeans and a jacket, and I'll pick you up at home? The temperature's not bad at all today, and the wind is calm."

She looked at him, then outside, where the setting sun gilded the chrome frame of the bike. "Okay."

"I'll give you fifteen minutes."

"Fifteen!"

"You want to get on the road before it's dark, don't you? Seeing a sunset from the back of a Harley is an experience you don't want to miss."

She straightened the items on her desk and

reached down to get her purse from the drawer. Case sneaked a peek at the doodling beneath the children's picture book.

She had written his name and initials, along with bold, swiggly lines and angry circles. Well, at least she'd been thinking of him. He eased the book back into position as she raised up.

"Ready?" he asked innocently.

"Yes. Fifteen minutes," she said, glancing at the sturdy watch on her dainty wrist. "I'll be ready."

"Good." He glanced outside, saw no one around, then leaned over the desk and kissed her before she could pull away.

He held her head lightly with one hand and whispered against her lips, "I missed you." Then he strode out the door before he upset their dinner plans by making love to her on the library checkout desk.

Mandy gasped as Case vroomed away from the curb. She dug her fingers beneath his leather jacket, into his hard stomach, and held on for dear life. Good heavens, had she ever believed this would be fun?

But then she opened her eyes and watched them speed past tree trunks and parked cars. This certainly wasn't his aunts' big sedan, nor her tame little compact. She breathed deeply, taking in the smells of fall with no hint of dampness. Mulberry and cottonwood leaves skittered across the pavement as if hurrying to get out of the Harley's path.

"Relax," Case said over his shoulder. Even though she heard him clearly, she used the wind and roar of the engine as an excuse to snuggle closer, resting her cheek against the soft leather that covered his back. At the same time, she eased her death grip on his waist, hoping she hadn't left permanent imprints in his flesh.

He turned right, coming off the town square, and she leaned with him, exhilarated by the sensation of nearly tipping over before the bike righted itself— with the aid of Case—and roared out of town. She gripped tighter with her legs, rubbing her jeans against his. The wind whipped past, taking her breath away. She snuggled behind Case and smiled into the increasing darkness.

He reached back and nudged her when they were past the auto repair shop and salvage yard, pointing to the west. The trees thinned out, and she saw the fading sunset through a break. Deep rose, yellow, and purple streaked the sky—horizontal lines that looked like thin jet vapor trails above the sun's orange glow. Smiling, she rested her chin against Case's shoulder and shouted into his ear, "Beautiful."

She should have tried riding a motorcycle years ago, she decided as they rode into the setting sun. But then, the experience wouldn't have been the same with another bike and another man. Case hadn't mentioned where they were going, and she hadn't asked. She trusted him, she realized, not just with her safety, but with her reputation.

The trip ended just as she was beginning to get chilly from the lower temperatures after the sun went down. She changed position to see where they were going. To her surprise, they'd arrived at a cozy restaurant in a remodeled cottage. Soft lamp light filtered through lacy curtains at the multi-paned windows.

"Where are we?" she asked as soon as he cut the engine.

"Mineola. Have you been here before?"

"To the town, yes," she said, easing her hands away from his hard stomach. "To this restaurant, no."

He swiveled around to look at her, his cheeks pink from the ride. "I discovered it the other day when I was riding around. I hope you like it."

"It looks great." She held on to his arm and swung her leg over the back of the bike. The ground seemed unsteady, as if they were in the midst of an earthquake, but she knew that her muscles and equilibrium were to blame.

Case swung off beside her, unaffected by the trip. "So, did you enjoy the ride?"

"Yes, very much." She smoothed her hair behind her ears. "I must look a mess."

"Just a little tousled." He finger combed her hair, then straightened her insulated jacket. "There. You look . . . great."

"Thank you." She broke eye contact, embarrassed, as always, by his compliments.

"Let's get inside. I'm suddenly hungry."

Within a few minutes, they were seated in what must have been the back bedroom of the cottage. The walls were papered in soft pink with yellow roses, and a small chandelier hung over their cream and pink draped table. Mismatched china and stemware added charm to the setting.

After their waitress left to get water for each of them Mandy leaned forward. "Case, this is lovely. I'm surprised you found this place."

"Because I'm a biker dude?" he asked, but his tone was teasing.

"No, because it looks secluded. I didn't know it was here."

"You probably would have learned if you'd been dating."

She shrugged. "I never got around to dating after I moved to Scottsville."

"I know. Greta and Millicent told me." Case folded his menu, smiled, then leaned closer, as though he was sharing a big secret. "See, even if you *don't* date, you still get talked about."

And speaking of big secrets, he owed her one. "Are you going to tell me what you've been hiding?"

"Yes." Case straightened, his smile vanishing. He looked very relieved when the waitress entered with glasses of water.

"Have you decided?" she asked.

"How about some wine?" Case asked.

"Wine?" Mandy wrinkled her nose. "I'm not sure I'm ready for any yet."

"They don't have dandelion wine, I'm sure. How about a glass of merlot?" He turned to their waitress. "Do you have merlot?"

"I'm not sure, sir. Let me check."

As soon as they were alone, Mandy returned to the subject. "So, about that secret . . ."

"Let's wait until after dinner. No need to get interrupted."

By the time the waitress cleared away the dinner plates and poured them coffee, Mandy was about ready to reach across the table and shake the secret out of Case. "Okay, no more excuses. Tell me."

"No dessert?"

"No! Now tell me. I'm imagining all kinds of things, and each one is more bizarre than the next."

"I don't think you've imagined this one," he said.

"Case!"

"All right. Now, I want to preface this with the understanding that I didn't actually lie to you about anything. What I told you about myself was true: I live in Colorado, not far from Estes Park; I've worked in various jobs in my life; I've driven a lot of different vehicles."

"You're not going to say you omitted the fact that you have a wife and two children back in Colorado, are you?"

"No, I told you I wasn't married and have never been married."

"Then what! You're not a felon, are you?"

"No, I'm a writer."

Mandy sat back in her chair, studying him as if seeing him for the first time. "A writer," she repeated, trying to see him as someone who spent long hours moving paragraphs around on a computer screen.

"Yes."

"Are you published?"

He nodded, then took a sip of his coffee. "Yes."

She tilted her head to the side, trying to understand why this was a huge secret . . . unless he was ashamed of his work. "What do you write?" She hoped he didn't say erotica or white supremacy handbooks or something equally outrageous.

"Mystery novels."

Mandy frowned. "Why haven't I heard of you?"

He shifted in his seat. "You have. I believe you mentioned I write particularly realistic and appealing female characters."

"I did?" She couldn't remember saying that about Case. He'd never shown her anything he'd written. The only conversation they'd had was about . . . "Oh, no. You're not telling me you're Casey Flannigan, are you?"

CHAPTER TEN

"Guilty as charged." Case searched Mandy's expression for something beyond shock, but found only confusion and disbelief. "I never told you I *wasn't* a writer."

Her eyes narrowed. "How do I know you're Casey Flannigan?"

"Casey is my birth name. Flannigan is my mother's maiden name. As for the rest, you can test me, or call my publisher. You may have spoken to Valerie Boyd about a book signing."

"Well, that certainly explains why she knew I wanted to have a book signing, and why Casey Flannigan already knew the date of the Harvest Festival and had made arrangements for a place to stay." She frowned. "I was having trouble figuring that one out."

"I didn't mean to confuse you."

"Why wouldn't you use your real name—I mean, Gardner?" She still looked skeptical.

"When I started writing, I was still working in Arizona as a speechwriter for a fairly prominent, very traditional politician. He wouldn't have appreciated letting the world in on my other profession, especially since I wrote murder mysteries. So I wrote my first three books while maintaining my anonymity. When I quit and moved to Colorado," he added with a shrug, "I didn't see the need to change."

"So you had the books sent, and then had the publicist call to arrange the book signing."

"I only meant to help."

"You were laughing at me, weren't you, when I came over to tell you about the books that I'd received. You knew all along they were coming, and not because of any letters the Friends of the Library sent out."

"Yes, I knew, but I was enjoying your excitement too much to allow reality to intrude. One thing I've learned, Mandy, is that writing lets you maintain a kind of control you rarely have in real life. I didn't see any harm in not telling you that I'd made a few calls to New York."

"You don't consider lying harmful?"

"I didn't consider keeping my identity from you as lying."

"You've been writing fiction too long, Case," Mandy accused, wadding her napkin into a ball and throwing it to the table. Agitated, she pushed her chair back and stood. Thankfully, they were the only diners in the small room. He knew she'd hate to make a scene in public.

"Maybe I have," he said gently, leaning back in his chair, "but I never considered my relationship with you anything other than real."

"How can I believe you?"

She paced the room, upset, but he knew going to her, enfolding her in his arms, wouldn't help. She'd pull away, and he didn't want to risk aggravating her further. Sometime in the last two days, he'd decided he needed Mandy in his life longer than two months. He'd been willing to be patient to get her into his bed; now he needed extra forbearance to convince her that they belonged together.

At the same time, he had to be willing to take risks.

"Mandy, do you believe me?"

She stopped pacing and faced him. "About what?"

"What I do for a living and why I didn't tell you earlier."

"It all makes sense—you being a writer, being able to buy an expensive motorcycle, coming to town to help your aunts, sending books to a small town library—but I still don't understand why you didn't tell me."

He pushed away from the table and walked slowly toward her, keeping eye contact. "Because I needed you to want me for who I was in Scottsville, not in New York City or Colorado. If I'd told you right away that I wrote books under the name Casey Flannigan, I would have never known."

"You don't . . . you can't be serious."

Her words spoke of doubts, but the hope he saw in her dark eyes made him believe this was going to work out. *Patience,* he told himself.

Their waitress came to the doorway, started to speak, and then left when he motioned her away. Case turned his attention back to the woman who had turned his world upside down in only two short weeks.

"Mandy, I joke around and tease you about a lot of things, but about this, I'm very serious." He reached for her hands, but she stepped back, out of reach.

"How could you? I went out of my way to be unattractive. I wasn't trying to invite anyone's attention."

Case shrugged. "Maybe that's what attracted me the most. I was intrigued from the start and wanted to know why a naturally beautiful woman would downplay her assets so much. I had to find out. When I finally got to know you better, there were other facets of your personality I had to explore."

"Case, you make me sound like some *femme fatale!* Even when I dressed in shorter skirts and higher heels, I wasn't the kind of woman you're describing. I think you're confusing fiction with reality."

"I'm not confused at all, but I know I've confused you. Just give me a chance, Mandy. Give *us* a chance." He longed to hold her tight, but couldn't force her to accept him. He only wished she would let him touch her, just for a moment.

She didn't retreat any farther, holding her ground with her pride intact. "What about when Greta is well again? I'm staying in Scottsville. I've made a commitment to this town to rebuild the library, and I'm going to see that through. I'm not going to get distracted again. I'm going to prove that I can make a difference."

"You are making a difference. I want to help."

She shook her head. "I think you want to take over."

"No, I don't. I have my own life, Mandy. I don't want to take over yours. I simply want to share it."

She looked at him a long time, her head slightly

tilted to one side. A single tear pooled in her eye, gilded gold by the soft lights of the dining room. Then, with a faint sigh of surrender, she took a small step toward him.

"Ah, Mandy." He closed the gap between them, folding her into his arms. She melted into him, clinging as tightly as when they'd roared toward the setting sun. She smelled of fresh air, a light floral cologne, and the unique fragrance of the old house that seemed to embrace them as they held each other.

"I'll give you a chance, Case Gardner, or Casey Flannigan, or whoever you are," she whispered against his chest. "Just don't expect me to change. I won't start wearing those uncomfortable shoes again."

Despite the emotions that felt too close to the surface, Case chuckled. "We're going to be fine, Mandy. I don't want to go back to suits and ties again, either."

She leaned back, looking at him incredulously. "You, in a tie?"

He touched the tip of her nose with his finger. "Boggles the mind, doesn't it?"

Eleven days later, the morning of the Harvest Festival dawned with fleeting gray rain clouds in the west, but soon turned sunny, which Case was pleased to see.

He felt some reservations about revealing his identity. He'd become a success without book signings or public appearances. Letting the world know who he was, even at a small town event like this, would change his status. His publisher had already talked about putting his photo on the next book. Case had laughingly suggested putting the Harley on there, too, and they'd jumped on the idea. He now faced the prospect of actually assuming the bad boy identity that Mandy had found so intriguing.

He hoped he wasn't creating a monster.

As he stood at the bakery's window and looked out on the decorated town square—harvest bouquets of corn and wheat swaying in the breeze—he wondered where Mandy was right now. A few workers were draping the platform that had been erected near the gazebo. He'd be signing books there later today, with Mandy alongside of him. He hoped she'd be whispering the names of Scottsville's citizens into his ear.

She'd worked herself to exhaustion planning the book signing. Although he'd been worried about the way she'd placed so much importance on this one event, she brushed off his concerns. Mandy, he realized, needed to be in control of her own life. When she felt out of control, she freaked. Putting up with a whole group of other people who didn't share her priorities left her out of control much of the time.

They hadn't spent much time together, and he missed her. He knew they would continue their relationship as soon as this fundraising event was finished. As a matter of fact, he'd made her promise that she'd take Sunday off. He hoped she'd agree to go to dinner with him tonight.

He was going to keep her to that promise, because his patience had come to an end. He wanted her, sensible shoes and all.

Mandy didn't enjoy speaking in public. She'd convinced Brenda Ayres, Jillian's sister-in-law, to do the duty of announcing the booksigning. Brenda had a lot of experience with volunteer activities, but Mandy wasn't sure how well the chatterbox could keep a secret. For that reason, she didn't reveal the identity of Casey Flannigan to anyone—even the woman who was going to call him to the stage.

The Harvest Festival brought in a big crowd this year. Small children with painted faces pulled their parents to the many booths set up around the square. Shoppers wandered from Ye Olde Tea Shoppe to the antiques and collectibles stores. Several businesses, including the bakery and pet store, had shut down for the day so that the owners and employees could attend the festival.

The bake sale was going well on the other side of the square. All the volunteers seemed to be doing their jobs. She only hoped she'd be able to carry out her responsibilities for the rest of the day without collapsing in a heap.

No one seemed to think it odd that Case stood near the gazebo, seemingly relaxed in his jeans, white T-shirt, and leather jacket. He hadn't shaved in two days, and the slight stubble only added to his faintly dangerous attractiveness. The delicate older lady on his arm seemed as out of place as a ballerina at a football game, but Millicent Gardner seemed blissfully ignorant of the picture they presented. She pointed out friends and neighbors as she smiled and waved.

Case smiled often at Millicent's comments, although Mandy thought he looked a little tense. But perhaps she was just projecting her own fears about how well he'd be received by the people already lining up to get their copy of *New Mexico Nomad,* his last hardcover mystery. He always seemed so cool and self-assured that she had trouble thinking of him as uncomfortable in any situation.

Brenda's voice over the speakers startled Mandy out of her contemplation. She didn't have any doubt Case would be fine; he always managed to come up with a clever response and a witty comeback.

"The time is now three o'clock and it's time for a book signing with our mysterious author, Casey Flannigan," Brenda announced. Her cheerleader-like voice rang out clearly around the town square. "Now, I know you all want a copy of his latest release," she said, holding up the book, "since all the proceeds benefit our library. Please form a line to the left of the platform, and we'll get started as soon as we get our mystery guest up here."

Brenda made a big show of placing her hand against her forehead as though she was shading her eyes. She looked dramatically around the crowd, drawing a few chuckles. "Casey Flannigan, if you're in the audience, please come forward and meet your fans."

Silence. Mandy held her breath as a few people shifted, looking around. Case patted Millicent's hand, then started walking. The crowd parted for him and the whispers began. A few people started clapping. By the time he made it to the platform, applause greeted him.

"Well, look at this!" Brenda said, her surprise genuine. "Our very own Case Gardner, nephew of Scottsville's favorite ladies, Greta and Millicent!" She leaned toward him and caught his arm, pulling him to the microphone.

Mandy thought Brenda was holding him too tight, looking at him too adoringly, for a married lady.

Perhaps she should get up there and see that Case wasn't manhandled too much by the friendly announcer.

"Are you really the bestselling author the world knows as Casey Flannigan?"

"Yes, I am," he said, smiling at the audience. Mandy noticed a few photographers, some of whom looked like pros, point their cameras at Case. "I'm sorry to say that my parents stuck me with the name 'Casey,' although I've always preferred 'Case.' And in honor of my mother, I wrote under her maiden name. Now that the secret's out, I'll just have to remember who I am when I pick up a pen to sign a copy of my book for you."

He ended his short announcement with a devil-may-care smile that had all the women moving closer to the stage. Mandy realized that she'd become accustomed to thinking of Case as hers somehow. She wasn't sure she liked sharing him with all those other women. They looked as though they'd like to take Case home to turn the pages of *New Mexico Nomad* for them.

She was jealous, she realized, not envious. She didn't want to be famous, nor did she want to brag that she knew Case, the famous author. She had a feeling she liked Case Gardner much more than Casey Flannigan. No, she wanted to lay claim to him in a very elemental way. She wanted to tell the world that he belonged to her.

Of course, he didn't. He looked good up there on the platform, taking a seat behind a table where he'd greet his fans. He would be doing more signings and travel more now that his secret had been revealed. Mandy could tell from talking to Valerie Boyd that she was thrilled he'd decided to go public. There would even be a photo of him on his Harley on the back of his next book. Case was going to be famous, a cross between John Grisham and George Clooney.

She would continue as a small town librarian, struggling with an inadequate budget. Her biggest creative challenge would be getting more people to use the library, while his would be writing books to fill the shelves.

They had little in common other than a love of books. Why would he want to stay in a town like Scottsville when he could live anywhere he wanted? New York, Los Angeles, or even on one of those ranches in Wyoming or Montana where his neighbor might be Harrison Ford or Robert Redford.

Mandy wasn't going to leave here, even if he asked, which she was sure he wouldn't. She would never be able to function in that type of hectic lifestyle. If Dallas held too many distractions for her—and on a librarian's salary, at that—how could she focus on improving herself if she had to travel and entertain? She vowed she wouldn't go back to being the unfocused, flighty person she'd been before.

No, Case would be here for only a short while. She would be here for many years, long after he'd gone on to fame and fortune.

"Mandy, we need you up here," Brenda called to her.

Indeed, the line was growing longer, and Mandy had duties to perform. With a sigh for what wasn't going to be, she headed for the platform where Case reigned supreme.

CHAPTER ELEVEN

The crowds started thinning out by five o'clock, and Case was glad. His hand actually hurt from signing so many books! Fortunately, his publisher had sent extras, because they had more faith in the number of readers he'd draw to Scottsville than he did. As he leaned back in his chair and stretched, he watched parents herd their weary children into the family car, truck, or van for the ride home. The Harvest Festival had been a success; the book signing had been a revelation.

He'd focused on how revealing his identity would affect *him*, but apparently he had a lot of fans out there who wanted to know details of his life: what he did before he became a writer, where he got his story ideas, if he was married or divorced, what he was doing next. He hadn't realized readers would be so interested in him, rather than just his books.

Mandy had done a super job letting the media

know about the fundraiser. Reporters and photographers had come from as far away as Shreveport and Dallas. Of course, Case didn't have time for in-depth interviews, but he'd promised to schedule one via phone for next week. Several readers had told him how far they'd driven to meet him after reading about the event in their local newspapers.

He stood, rolled his shoulders beneath the leather jacket, and looked around for Mandy. Clouds were gathering in the west, so there would be no beautiful sunset. He didn't need nature to cooperate with his plans tonight; he simply needed Mandy's agreement to go to dinner. He'd take the rest of the evening from there.

He spotted her across the square, talking to the Patterson family. He'd met them in the bakery and around town, and knew Mandy liked Jillian. He also knew she secretly wanted a puppy, but hadn't done anything about getting herself a pet. One more mystery about Mandy that he might solve someday.

He walked toward her, watching how the breeze molded her skirt to her legs and bottom, the way she constantly smoothed her hair behind her ears, even though the wind seemed intent on curving the strands around her face. She hadn't seen him yet, and her happy smile and easy gesture told Case she was relaxed and open.

He hoped she would continue to enjoy the success of the fundraiser. Now, if she could put that behind her for a night, he'd be a happy man. The time had come to be together without the library or his identity coming between them.

The Pattersons said their goodbyes, and Mandy turned around. She spotted him immediately. Her eyes widened just a little, telling him that she still enjoyed looking at him. He hoped she had the opportunity to look her fill later. He was more than ready to see what she was hiding beneath those frumpy clothes.

"Finished for the day?" he asked.

"I think so. Everyone seems to have enjoyed the festival, and I've already taken care of the bank deposit from the booksigning."

"Good. Then would you like to get some dinner?"

She tilted her head slightly. "Yes, dinner would be good. Where would you like to go?"

"I was thinking about Tyler," he said casually. He stepped closer, and when she didn't seem surprised or alarmed, he put his arm across her left shoulder and rubbed her neck. "You've worked hard. You deserve a break."

"I promised I'd take tomorrow off."

"I'd like to take it off with you."

"Well . . . I'd like that."

"I think we should take it off together . . . in Tyler."

She swallowed. "Tomorrow?"

"How about starting tonight?"

"What? Oh, you mean . . ."

"Staying over."

"Together?"

"Yes." He placed his other hand on her right shoulder and rubbed her tense muscles. "Definitely together, at a hotel, in one room. I think we know each other well enough now, don't you?"

"I suppose so," she answered in little above a whisper.

"Mandy, we don't have to do anything if you don't

want to. I'm just being honest with you. I'm more than ready."

She swallowed again, then straightened and looked him in the eye. "I'm ready, too."

He smiled, even though he'd felt as though he'd just touched a live wire. "You are, hmm?"

"Yes."

"Then why are we standing around in the town square when we could be someplace private, getting naked?"

Her shocked expression made him laugh out loud, but he simply pulled her close and headed towards her car.

After being the center of attention most of the day, the anonymity of dining in Tyler was sweet, indeed. Case found a Thai restaurant in a shopping center on the south side of the loop. Mandy had never eaten Thai food before and had heard it was very spicy, but she trusted Case not to order anything that would fry her tastebuds.

Especially when she'd boldly reminded him that she had other uses for her tongue later that night.

They fed each other tasty morsels of chicken, vegetables, and mystery delicacies Case wouldn't identify. They laughed over glasses of crisp, white wine that complimented the spicy food. When it was finally time to leave, Mandy knew the warm glow didn't come only from the cuisine.

With few words between them, Case drove her car to one of the few large, nice hotels in town. She waited uncomfortably in the reception area while he checked in. If she thought about what she was doing—what they would soon be doing—she might wimp out. But she wanted to be with Case, even if they only had a short time before he went back to his "other" life.

She'd come inside rather than hiding in the car because she wanted to prove to him that she wasn't afraid of being seen in his company. Of course, there wasn't much chance of seeing a Scottsville resident in a hotel in Tyler . . . unless someone else was getting ready to have a hot and heavy affair, too.

She and Case had about five weeks left, she realized as she watched two other couples enter the hotel, laughing and having fun. She didn't want to spend her short time with Case nursing doubts and fears. She wanted memories.

"Ready?" he asked, surprising her. For a big man who wore boots, he could be remarkably quiet.

She nodded and swung the strap of her overnight case to her shoulder. He took her hand and led her toward the elevator.

"You're nervous," he said as he punched the button. He looked at her gently as his fingers massaged her hand.

"A little. I'm not used to doing this."

"I know. Despite that bad-boy image I'm supposed to promote, I'm not into bed-hopping. And I haven't been involved in a relationship for nearly a year. Just so you'll know, I'm also okay medically. I've had all my shots and vaccinations and tests and I got a clean bill of health."

Mandy smiled. "I'm glad to know I won't get rabies if you bite me."

The doors to the empty elevator opened. "Bite you? Why, Miss Mandy!" Case said in a shocked tone that made her laugh. "I'm thoroughly surprised at you."

"As long as you aren't disappointed," she said as they stepped inside.

"No chance of that," he said, dropping his bag and pulling her close, "unless you bolt out of this hotel right now."

"No chance of that," she echoed, tilting her mouth up to his as the elevator doors slid shut.

Somehow, Case managed to push the button to their floor before their kiss turned fiery. She ran her fingers through his long hair, tugging him closer, as his tongue claimed her mouth. There were too many layers of clothing between them, she realized as she pressed close. She wanted to feel his warm flesh, and nothing else, against her own.

By the time the elevator stopped and the doors slowly opened, Mandy was ready to pull Case's T-shirt from his jeans, slide her hands up his broad back, and wrap a leg around his. She wanted to be bold and sexy, but she hadn't done anything like this in a long time. The truth was, she felt as nervous as if this were the first time.

"Slow down," he whispered against her lips. "At least let's find our room."

"Good idea." She repositioned her overnight case on her shoulder with one hand and grabbed him with the other. "What's the number?"

Case's chuckle made her turn around. "What's so funny?"

"Mandy, when you have a change of heart, you go for the full one-eighty, don't you?"

"I'm determined to be more decisive." *Especially*

where you're concerned, she added silently. "But if it would make you feel better, lead the way."

"To your right," he said, picking up his own bag. "Six-twenty-one." He looped his free arm around her shoulders. "And there's nothing to be nervous about. We know each other pretty well. You do trust me, don't you?"

"Oh, yes, I trust you. And I'm not really nervous."

"You're not?" he asked, inserting the card key into the lock.

"Well, maybe a little," she said, pausing at the doorway to their room.

"If you'd rather not—"

"No! I'm ready." Physically, that was so true. She felt hot and pleasantly achy in all the right places. Only when she thought about Case leaving did her heart hurt so bad she wasn't sure she could stand it. Making love wasn't going to make it hurt any less.

She could survive his leaving. She'd endured separations before. She'd said goodbye to friends and lovers.

Not like Case, her little voice reminded her.

"Mandy?"

She shook her head. "Sorry. I zoned out for a minute. I was thinking . . . too much."

"I'm glad you're the one who said that," he teased. "Come on. Let's see if we can pick up where we left off."

She smiled reassuringly—and preceded him into the room. Illumination from the hallway revealed a kingsize bed that seemed as large as the platform where he'd signed books that afternoon. She dropped her overnight case, purse, and jacket on the dresser, and was just about to make some witty comment when she heard the click as he shut and locked the door and the thunk of his own bag being dropped.

He came up behind her, slipping his arms around her waist and pulling her tight against his body. He must have shed his leather jacket, because she felt his soft T-shirt against her thin blouse. "I've wanted to undress you from the first time I saw you."

"You have?"

"Absolutely." His hands moved up, over her ribs and the undersides of her breasts, finally cupping her. "I wondered what you were hiding beneath these baggy clothes. Whether your underwear was plain cotton or thin and silky. Whether all your skin was as smooth and flawless as your face."

"I'm nothing special," she whispered. "I hope you aren't expecting to find a centerfold lurking underneath."

Case chuckled, his breath warm against her hair and neck as he rubbed her nipples to peaks. "You're the real thing. Don't you realize I couldn't care less about your cup size? I'm just curious, that's all, and it's driving me crazy."

She reached back and stroked his upper arms, his shoulders, wherever she could reach. "Then maybe you should do something to satisfy your curiosity."

"If that's an invitation, I'm accepting."

His nimble fingers worked on the buttons of her white blouse, his hand brushed against her breasts in the most tantalizing manner. With his other arm, he pressed her tighter against his arousal. He was working the buttons so slowly. She wanted to feel his flesh against hers, but she couldn't urge him to hurry, not when what he was doing felt so good.

He parted the prim blouse with both hands, again

skimming over her breasts. Her nipples pebbled hard, pressing against her bra, and she caught her breath.

"Hmm. Silky," he whispered. "Now let's see what's beneath this skirt."

Thankful she'd been exercising fairly regularly, she leaned her head back against his shoulder and rubbed whatever part of him she could reach: his arms, his thigh, his butt. Her zipper sighed as he worked it down. Within seconds, her skirt fell to the floor.

"Much better," Case said, turning her in his arms, studying her with a possessive gaze, "but you're still wearing too many clothes."

"So are you." She pulled his T-shirt from his jeans and slid her hands up his warm, smooth back. His muscles seemed to shift beneath her hands, stretching like a big cat being stroked. She loved the feel of him and the heat he generated.

She wanted more.

Her fingers opened the button on his jeans, then the zipper. His arousal bulged against his cotton briefs.

"Case," she whispered, stroking him through his unzipped jeans.

"Not yet. My turn." He knelt, pulling her pantyhose down. She wished she'd worn something sexier, but she hadn't because of the festival. However, he didn't seem to care. Now the hose were gone.

Then his lips were on her stomach, flirting with her navel, driving her crazy. She sank her hands into his hair and pulled him closer. In one smooth motion, he reached behind her and flicked open her bra. With another flip, it sailed across the room.

"Better," he said, looking up into her eyes. Then his gaze began to roam down her neck, to her breasts, to her stomach, and back again. His hands did the same, molding her to him, driving her crazy with a touch both gentle and demanding.

Mandy reached for the bottom of his T-shirt. "Your turn." She stripped the garment over his head, throwing it in the direction of her bra.

After she'd looked her fill at his impressive chest, she ran her hands over him, snuggled her breasts just below his heart, and nestled close. Nothing had ever felt so right. She held him tight, and he returned the embrace, lifting her from the floor and rubbing her whole body against his. She took advantage of the position to kiss him, deeply, urgently. She couldn't get enough of the taste and feel of this man.

Without a word, he guided her toward the bed. He eased her down on the dark bedspread and kissed her again. When he raised his head, she gasped for breath and reached for him.

"In a moment," he whispered. In jerky movements, he removed his boots, socks, and, finally, his jeans. He pulled several packets from his wallet before tossing it aside, too. Then he was beside her again, stripping off her panties, leaving her naked.

"This isn't right," he said, gazing at her with feverish eyes.

"What?"

Without a word, he picked her up as though she weighed almost nothing. She stood on shaky legs as he jerked back the coverlet, blanket, and top sheet. Only after lying her back on the bed, spreading her hair out against the whiteness, did he smile. "You're so beautiful, you make me forget all the words I have inside me. I can't write anything as lovely as you are right now."

She nearly cried. Instead, she pulled his head down and kissed him, showing him all the love she felt in her heart. She tugged at his briefs until he swept them away, too. Now nothing separated them, at least nothing physical.

He sheathed himself and knelt between her thighs. But Case was rarely predictable, even when she wanted nothing more than to feel him move inside her. He lifted her gently with his hands on her bottom.

"Hold on," he said simply, then guided her to him until she surrounded him. He entered her smoothly and relentlessly. She buried her face in his chest, whispered his name, and clenched around him.

With a groan, he began to move. She went with him, down to the bed, rolling to the side, straddling him. She strained, reveling in the feel of him deep inside of her, holding him, wanting him. She moaned as the first waves shook her and cried out when she reached the crest.

His cry followed hers as they sank to the sweat-dampened sheets, legs entwined, arms holding tight. She sank into the sweet oblivion of passion, wondering how she would ever let him go.

Case awoke before six o'clock the next morning, accustomed to getting up before dawn to drive Millicent to the bakery. Funny how a person could get into a habit in only four weeks. Funny how one's world could change by walking into a small town library and finding a woman like Mandy hiding beneath baggy clothes and a no-nonsense attitude.

She lay on her stomach, sprawled across the bed in

abandon, sleeping as though exhausted. She probably was. She wanted so badly to do everything right: put on the proper appearance; say the correct response; make no errors in her work. He wondered what her parents had done to make her believe she was less than wonderful.

She didn't talk about her past. Hell, they hadn't had much time to talk at all in the last ten days, and before that, the only opportunity had been when he'd given her too much dandelion wine. Her remarks about finding solace in the library were telling, especially since he'd felt the same way.

They needed to talk about both their pasts and their future. He knew she still didn't believe he'd be happy with her or Scottsville in the long run, but he'd been doing a lot of thinking about how they could work things out. There had to be a way. He didn't want to give up everything of his former life; he loved his cabin in Colorado, and he loved to travel.

He knew going public with his identity would change things. His publisher had been after him for the last two books to start promoting himself. He'd have media appearances, speaking engagements— everything he'd blissfully avoided for the past six years.

He looked at Mandy's face, relaxed in sleep. An angel on the outside, a pretty darn demanding devil on the inside, he remembered with a grin. He had believed her when she told him she didn't mess around, that she hadn't gone to bed with anyone in a long time. She might not be the most experienced woman in the world, which was fine with him, but she did have a natural aptitude that took his breath away.

They would find a way to work out their differences.

Case leaned down and kissed her forehead, making her grumble and turn the other way. He grinned again. He'd better get out of bed before he deprived her of some much needed sleep. Poor baby. He'd made her promise to rest, then they'd kept each other up half the night.

He felt around the floor for his discarded T-shirt and jeans, then grabbed his shaving things and quietly retreated to the bathroom. He'd get some coffee and breakfast and then come back and see if Mandy was awake.

When Mandy awoke, she was alone. She ran her hand over the sheet and pillow, but they were cold.

"Case?"

No answer. He'd left her to sleep, but she didn't feel as rested as she did deserted. She'd wanted to waken beside him, to know the wonder of snuggling into his arms, still sleepy and sated from last night.

But he'd left some time ago, apparently. Why did such a simple thing hurt so much?

You're being too sensitive, she told herself. But she couldn't help feeling very alone in the hotel room.

She'd spent all of the last night exploring Case: his body, his reactions to her hands and mouth, his deep moans and rich laugh.

If she felt like this after only one night, how was she going to survive when he left Scottsville?

Unwilling to lie around, getting more and more depressed over Case's ultimate departure from her life, she rolled out of bed. Her body ached deliciously from his passionate lovemaking. She smelled like a woman who had been thoroughly and completely satisfied. She wouldn't use the word "loved." Neither one of them had mentioned it last night, so why delude herself in the light of day?

She needed a warm shower and something to take her mind off of him.

She'd just adjusted the water to the right temperature and stepped under the stream when she heard a sound from the room. It wouldn't be the maid; the "Do Not Disturb" sign was on the door, thanks to Case. He'd probably returned from wherever he'd gone early this morning. A part of her wanted to know what kind of mood he'd be in today; another part of her didn't want to face him after all the intimacies they'd shared.

But her decision was taken away from her when the shower curtain was pulled back and a grinning, very naked Case stepped into her shower.

"I had this feeling you needed me," he said, taking the hotel-size bottle of shampoo from her.

"Needed you?" Wanted him, perhaps, if she let herself think about it.

"Sure. How can you possibly shampoo your hair and wash your back without me?"

How, indeed? Mandy pushed her doubts aside for the moment and gave herself up to his magic hands.

CHAPTER TWELVE

The library had never been more popular. As a result of last weekend's book signing, the temporary building had been cramped for space on Monday as children came with parents after school and older residents and stay-at-home moms visited. The hour or so after lunch and before school let out should be the slowest time of day, Mandy predicted.

The new books were all checked out, but with the renewed interest in reading, Mandy was certain people would bring the books back quickly for another selection.

The Gardner bakery was more popular, too, she noticed, standing at the front window and looking across the square. Case had complained he barely had time to mix and bake because of all the requests to sign earlier books of his that people brought in from their homes. She could tell he missed the quiet morning hours with Millicent and the other regulars, but at the same time, Mandy had to believe he enjoyed knowing how popular he was. He might not write the kind of book that appeared on Oprah's Book Club, but he sure entertained hundreds of thousands of readers.

He'd even hinted at a movie deal for his upcoming release when they'd shared dinner with Greta and Millicent last night.

Wow, Case in Hollywood. The thought boggled her mind, to use his phrase. The media would be more likely to believe he was the leading man rather than the writer. There was no telling how many beautiful, glamorous women he'd meet in California, especially now that he was becoming semi-famous.

She turned away from the window and took her seat at the check-in desk, resting her chin on her hand. The vision of him attending a Hollywood premiere of the movie made from his book, a blonde on one arm and a redhead on the other, made her cringe. Not that she wanted to dress in those designer gowns and endure hundreds of flashes, she told herself. She was a small town librarian, not some Hollywood hanger-on.

A mother and preschooler pulled up to the library in a Volvo. Time to quit daydreaming and get back to work. With a sigh, Mandy headed for her desk. At least within the walls of the library, there were few surprises. Nothing she couldn't handle.

Not at all like that wickedly handsome man who'd stolen her heart.

Case had counted the hours until he could go to Mandy's house on Tuesday. She'd invited him for dinner, a first in their relationship. Although he found her invitation sweet and thoughtful, he was much more interested in a "second" in their relationship—a repeat of that night at the hotel.

He felt like a teenager on a hormone high. As he cut the engine on the Harley, he couldn't keep a smile off his face as he thought about the evening ahead. Mandy had been tired last night, yawning discreetly after dinner with Greta and Millicent. He'd invited her so that they could be together, like a family. He liked that. But he'd realized dinner was all they were going to share. Mandy needed to catch up on the sleep she'd lost Saturday night, when she should have been resting, and Sunday, when a previous commitment at church had kept her out late. Two days, and he couldn't wait to touch her again.

"Evening, son."

Case looked across the street. Mr. Potter, the elderly theater owner, was fighting a losing battle with the leaves from two giant sycamore trees. The wind picked them up and blew them into his neighbor's yard nearly as fast as the man could rake them into a pile.

"Evening, Mr. Potter."

"You write another book yet?"

"I'm working on one, sir. Every afternoon."

"Good. I'm reading the one I bought on Saturday. Kind of slow, though, because the darn print's so small."

"I'll mention that to my publisher."

"You do that, son." The older man went back to raking.

Case started to knock, then noticed Mandy standing just inside the screen door. He pushed it open and slipped inside. "So much for keeping our relationship quiet."

"I gave up on that idea," she said with a shake of her head. "There are no secrets in a small town, I've been told."

"At least I'm more respectable now." He leaned down and kissed Mandy's soft lips.

"You know that's not why I'm resigned to admitting our relationship. Biker or author, you're still a single man, coming to a single woman's house." She shrugged. "I'm just hoping my neighbors won't be too critical."

"Don't worry. I've told everyone who stops by the bakery that I'm courting you."

Her eyes grew wide before she swallowed. "Courting? Isn't that a bit old-fashioned?"

"I suppose, but that's what it feels like."

Even in the growing darkness, he could tell she was blushing. "I never know when you're kidding and when you're serious, so I'm going to assume you're teasing me again."

"Assume whatever you want, sweetheart. I know exactly what I'm after."

Deciding to change the subject, he sniffed the air. "What's that I smell?"

"Kind of a Chinese skillet dinner. I don't have a wok, but I like to sauté chicken and vegetables. I figured you'd like it since you enjoyed the Thai food."

"Smells great. I didn't know you cooked."

"Not well, but I don't starve."

He looped an arm around her shoulders and guided her down the short hallway. "See what a team we make? You cook the entrees, I bake the desserts. Our children will never go hungry."

She smiled up at him, but didn't look as happy as he thought she would. As a matter of fact, she looked nervous, or thoughtful. He hoped nothing serious was bothering her. He couldn't stand the idea of Mandy fretting over any problems, but getting into a serious conversation at the moment didn't sound like a good idea, either. Cooks liked to serve meals when they were perfect, rather than hours late. And from his parents, he'd learned never to argue at the table.

He stopped at the doorway into the kitchen and pulled her close. "Are you sure you're okay? You seem a little tense."

She looked into his eyes, then glanced away. "I'm fine," she said with false cheer. "I had a really busy day, though. The library is now very popular."

"I'm glad you're getting more patrons, but you should have told me if you're too tired. I could have brought dinner over, or we could have postponed our evening."

"No, that's okay. I wanted to see you."

He tipped her chin up with his finger. "You're sure?"

"Case, really, I'm fine." She pushed away gently. "I'd better get dinner on the table before it gets cold."

"Okay," he said, letting her go. His arms felt empty, his mind unsettled. Something more than a busy day was bothering Mandy.

They made it through dinner with small talk about the people in town, about how well his writing was coming. The conversation made him think of couples who had been married for years, but he also knew a darker undercurrent flowed between them. He suspected she was simply waiting for the right time.

"Mandy, what's wrong?" he asked as they took a cup of coffee to the living room.

She took a deep breath. "This is hard for me to talk about, but I realize that I have to try to make you understand."

"What?" He wanted to lean closer, touch her, but she looked too damn fragile.

"You remember when I told you how unfocused I'd been when I was younger, until I left that life behind and moved to Scottsville?"

"Of course."

"We haven't talked about where our relationship is going, but sometimes I think that maybe you want to continue seeing me."

"I don't want to stop seeing you, if that's what you mean. We only met a few weeks ago, but I feel like I've known you forever. On the other hand, I realize there's a lot we don't know about each other."

"Exactly."

"As far as I'm concerned, Mandy," he said, stroking her hair, lingering on the line of her jaw, "we know the important things." He took a deep breath. "I started falling in love with you the minute I saw you in the library, surrounded by boxes, looking so adorably confused when you realized I wasn't a ten-year-old boy on a bicycle."

She closed her eyes as though she was in pain. When she opened them, tears shimmered.

"Mandy, don't cry," he said, cupping her head, wanting to pull her close and comfort her.

"No, wait." She pulled away. "I need to tell you this." She took a deep breath. "How could I not fall for you, too? You were everything exciting and all that I'd decided was forbidden." She smiled sadly. "You were a hot fudge sundae with extra whipped cream, and I was on a severe diet."

"Everyone needs to indulge themselves once in a while." He tried to sound light, but he supposed he failed when she continued.

"That's what you were . . . are, I'm afraid. You're a craving, an indulgence, a special treat. A person can't live on hot fudge sundaes."

"I think there's a little more to me than whipped cream." He didn't want to get angry at how she was looking at their relationship, but he felt frustrated— and maybe a little hurt—that she'd described him as the male equivalent of a bimbo.

"Oh, there's so much more," she assured him. "You're smart, clever, and talented. And you look," she paused, her luminous gaze roaming his body briefly before returning to his face, "so good you make my heart hurt and my body ache."

"Then what's wrong? We admire each other. We care for each other. I can't think of a better start to any relationship."

"That is the problem! We have a wonderful start, but I'm so afraid we have no finish, no end. Case, I can't live in your world."

"My what? What are you talking about?"

"The travel, the excitement. You mentioned the movie deal. The thought of visiting Hollywood and mingling with those people fills me with dread."

"Mandy, you're worrying for no reason. You're wonderful with people. Everyone loves you. And yes, I'd like for you to share whatever good things happen to me, but I'd never force you to be somewhere or do something you weren't comfortable with."

"Case, I need my orderly life! I need the comfort of routine. I love the fact that I'm helping rebuild this library, making a difference in this community. I can't give that up."

"I'm not asking you to, sweetheart. But we can work out the details. I'll hire someone to take care of the library while you're on a trip with me. You can come back to your library, to the people here who need you. You can have the best of both worlds."

"I . . . I don't want both worlds, Case," she said, the pain in her voice so acute he pushed aside his growing panic. "I can't live in your world. If I try, I'll become like I was before: frivolous and unfocused. I'll never get anything accomplished in my life."

"Mandy, that's silly. Of course you can. I don't want to take you away from what you love."

"You're not listening to me!" She jumped up and started pacing the room. "I need order. I need to avoid the very things you're dangling before me."

He walked toward her, wanting to fold her in his arms, wanting to pretend this conversation had never started. He wanted to go back to this weekend, when everything had been perfect, and the future stretched before them as a long, exciting adventure.

"Mandy, please don't do this to yourself . . . to us. We can work this out."

"How?" She hugged her arms around herself, looking so forlorn he wanted to hold her next to his body and make her stop talking about her doubts and fears.

"If we care for each other . . . dammit, if we love each other, we can work anything out!"

"Love doesn't conquer all," she whispered, her eyes filling with tears. "Case, I know what I need."

"Why, Mandy? Why is this need for focus and order more important than what we feel for each other?"

"You make it sound like I've suddenly decided something stupid and arbitrary. This is who I am, Case," she said, holding her arms out, her face filled with pain and frustration.

"I don't think you're being stupid or arbitrary. I think you're putting too much importance on something that might not be a problem. You might love to travel, and I might not get a movie deal. My success as an author might be gone in a year, or in five." He stepped closer, needing to make her understand. "What we have, Mandy, is stronger than a career. I want to believe it will last far longer than success or fame."

"Maybe it will," she said shakily, "but that doesn't mean I can be with you."

"You're leaving me for what *might* happen?"

"No, I'm saying there's no future for us because of who I am. Do you want me to start hating myself again when I start flitting from one project to the next, one interest to another? What does that say about my character, Case? How can I live with myself if I don't become the kind of person who can accomplish something in her life?"

"Mandy, you've already accomplished lots of things: your education, your career, this library. You're making friends in town. You've certainly captured my heart. There's lots ahead for you."

She shook her head. "I know myself, Case. I won't be anything if I don't stay focused on what I want."

"That's ridiculous! I know you're not a flake, Mandy!"

"I am. You just don't want to see that part of me."

"You're normal! Everyone has their moments. Besides, what's so wrong about having diverse interests? Think of all the skills you've acquired, all the fun—"

"Life is not about fun!" She turned away, into herself, to a place he was afraid he couldn't reach.

He stood perfectly still and carefully asked, "Why, Mandy? Who said life wasn't about having fun?"

"It just isn't! You'll never be serious about anyone. About me. I knew you wouldn't understand." She turned around, tears falling down her cheeks. "Please, just go. You're everything that's fun and creative and daring. But I'm not. I . . . I do love you, Case, but I'm not the woman for you. I can't live in your world."

"So you're pushing me out of yours."

"I must."

"No, Mandy," he said, walking toward the door, grabbing his leather jacket from the back of a chair. "You're afraid. If I thought I could . . . but I don't think you're ready to listen."

She closed her eyes and hugged her arms around herself. With one last look, he opened the door and slipped out into the night.

CHAPTER THIRTEEN

After four days of misery, unable to stop thinking about Case and how she'd pushed him out of her life, Mandy knew she had to resolve the issues from her past. She dreaded looking at herself critically, but she feared one thing more—losing the man she loved.

He'd tried to call this week, but she'd ignored his pleas to pick up the phone. His messages on her answering machine brought tears to her eyes, but still she hadn't relented.

With a sigh, she settled on her bed to think. She'd stepped into the role of a small-town librarian—a position she'd assumed would make her both content and productive—yet was she happy? No. Throughout her life, she tried to be the daughter her parents wanted, and failed. She'd tried to be the bright and cheerful friend, always ready to party, and nearly flunked out of school. She'd tried to conform to a

boring job with no real goal, and had ended up finding dozens of more interesting things to do with her
time.

Now, for the first time, she had a concrete goal—
rebuilding the library. She had good friends, a neat
and cozy house, and a future here, and yet her heart
called out for Case, and her little voice kept whispering in her ear, "Are you going to settle for being
miserable when you could have the man you love?"

She'd convinced herself if she dressed right and
looked right, she'd act right. But she was a grown
woman! Who was to say what was right or wrong? Her
parents, so unlike her in temperament? Her friends,
with their own goals and interests? Or herself, now
that she was an adult?

She pushed up from the bed, then opened the
doors of her closet. In the back, buried beneath extra
blankets and pillows, was a box of old favorites—
clothes she hadn't parted with when she'd acquired
the new, sensible, boring wardrobe. And to go with
them, shoes that flattered her feet.

Just the attire for a woman with a tattoo on her
butt.

She grabbed the box and ripped open the lid.
Everything smelled a bit musty, but she pulled them
out anyway. Mandy Thompson wasn't some sexless,
wimpy shell of a woman waiting for old age to catch
up with her. No! She was smart and sexy, and she
had a goal.

As soon as she told herself those stirring words, she
sank to the hardwood floor. Her goal. Only rebuilding
the library, or rebuilding herself, too? Had she put
all her energy into the small, unloved, sadly neglected
library because it was a symbol of herself?

"Yes," she whispered. "That's exactly what I've done."

Case let the phone ring until Mandy's answering machine picked up; then he replaced the receiver with a curse.

"What's wrong, dear?" Millicent asked as she entered the kitchen to fix a cup of herbal tea for herself and Greta.

"Mandy's what's wrong," he growled. "She's not answering, and I've already left two messages. I swear, I'm not going to beg anymore."

"You've been begging? Whatever for?"

"Oh, she's got some foolish notion that she has to be this picture-perfect woman, this paragon of virtue. She thinks that if she gets involved in my life, she'll mess up hers. All she wants is order, and she thinks I'm nothing but chaos."

"Oh, you're not chaotic," Millicent said, patting his arm despite the fact he was pacing like some caged animal and gesturing like a wild man. "You're just unique, like Greta and me. We always did have that in common, you know." His aunt chuckled as though what she'd said made sense.

"You and Greta aren't exactly what I'd call wild and crazy women, Aunt Millie," he pointed out in case she'd forgotten they were his elderly maiden aunts.

"Well of course we aren't wild! How would that look, carrying on at our age?" She filled her cup from the steaming pot, then added a tea bag. "But in our day, we were considered quite unconventional."

Before he could ask what she meant by that comment, she continued. "Now, what are you going to do about Mandy? You simply must get back into her good graces."

"Aunt Millie, she kicked me out. She said we didn't have a future. She won't talk to me."

"Did you tell her you loved her?"

"Pretty much. I told her I starting falling for her the minute I saw her."

"That's not a good answer, Case. No wonder you're still a bachelor!" She dipped her tea bag one last time before placing it in the trash. "Did you ask her to marry you?"

"No, but I said I wanted to be with her. That we had a future together."

"For heaven's sake! Why didn't you just get down on one knee and pop the question, as they say?"

His aunt took her herbal tea, patted his cheek, and walked from the room. Case sank into a chair, trying to remember why he hadn't just "popped the question." For starters, he needed a ring. And he really would love to show Mandy how much he cared. . . .

"Casthe," Mandy said, pulling open the door, unlatching the screen door.

He frowned as he stepped inside. "What's wrong with your voice?"

"Pheanut buhtter," she mumbled, desperately trying to dislodge the bite from her palate. "Oh, the heck wif it." She threw her arms around his neck and hugged him tight.

"Mandy," he said, grasping her arms and moving her back slightly so he could look into her eyes, "you're okay, right?" He pulled her close, holding her against his rapidly beating heart.

She worked the peanut butter loose and swallowed. "I'm fine. I was just having a sandwich."

"I got worried when you didn't return my calls, even though I told myself to give you some space."

"I had to think." She pulled back, wanting to tell him everything at once. "You were right: I was trying to live up to everyone else's expectations. I could never really be happy that way."

"And now?" he asked, his look intent as he stared at her.

She took a deep breath. "I know I could never be happy without you."

"Ah, Mandy," he whispered, his lips moving toward hers, "that was exactly the right answer."

He kissed her possessively, as though he wanted them to merge together and never part. He probed and she responded with a passion remembered from last weekend. It felt so eternal, she couldn't imagine she'd known him only a month.

He broke the kiss with little nibbles along her jaw, butterfly kisses to her eyelids. "You *have* been eating peanut butter," he whispered against her ear.

She laughed, holding him close. "I hope you like peanut butter."

"Love it." He smoothed her hair behind her ears and smiled down at her. "Love you."

Tears filled her eyes as the emotional ups and downs of this past week rushed to the surface. "I love you, too. I was afraid of telling you, convinced that if I didn't say the words, letting you go would be less painful."

"I didn't want you to let me go. I should have told you how I felt and asked you to marry me."

"Case," she said, stroking his jaw, "if you had asked me, the answer would have been the same. I wouldn't have said yes a week ago. I couldn't imagine living in your world, and I couldn't imagine you living in mine."

"And now? What do see for our future?"

"Compromise, as you suggested before. And understanding."

"Good answer." He kissed her again, his lips warm and firm as they lingered. He raised his head. "And what about the other question?"

"Which one?"

"If I asked you today, would you marry me?"

She started to answer, but he put his fingers to her lips and stopped her.

"No, wait. I want to do this right." He took her hand and pulled her toward the couch.

"Now who's being the traditionalist?" she teased, amused at his earnest attitude and intent expression. She was trying to "lighten up," but Case was becoming more serious by the second.

"Sit here," he said, pulling her down in the center of her couch.

He turned away for a moment, thrusting his hands in his jeans pockets. She sat and admired his rear. Very nice. She could get used to looking at him without much hardship at all.

He turned around, his face chiseled and stern, but his eyes glowing with emotion. "I've never done this before."

"That's okay. There's a first time for everything, as you told me once."

He went down on one knee, reached for her hand, then realized he had the wrong one. Taking a deep breath, he looked into her eyes. "Mandy, I love you. I know you love this town, and the library, and I promise never to take you away unless you want to go. I promise to be considerate when I travel, which I will have to do occasionally. I'll be supportive and I'll never underestimate the importance of your feelings again," he said, reaching into his pocket. He pulled out a ring that glimmered in the lamp light. "I promise all that, if you'll do me the honor of becoming my wife."

The tears that had threatened moments ago spilled from her eyes. Case seemed to shimmer and shift before her gaze, almost as if he was a mirage. She reached out, needing to feel his strong shoulders.

"Mandy? Say something."

She realized he was holding the ring, ready to place it on her finger. She held out her hand and whispered, "Yes."

Case let out a deep breath, then smiled and slid the ring on her finger. The round diamond sparkled, winking back at her. Very traditional, very beautiful.

"It's wonderful, Case," she said softly. "I would have been happy with a simple gold band."

"You'll get one. I'm thinking of a Christmas wedding."

"Christmas, hmm? What if I want to be a June bride?"

"You want to wait that long before we can live together under one roof? Before we can make love without wondering who's going to find out?"

"Good point. Christmas sounds great. Something small, okay?"

"You're sure? I've already called the Mormon Tabernacle."

She laughed at his teasing. Her old Case was back. And he really loved her.

"How about a simple service with only close friends and family?"

He settled on the couch next to her. "Speaking of families, will yours be okay with your decision?"

"Yes, they'll be fine. I finally accepted the fact that I am my own person, with my own needs and goals. And you're the man I love. They'll have to accept you, too."

Case smiled, his eyes glowing with love and, if she wasn't mistaken, passion. "I like that outfit."

"This old thing?"

"Um-hmm." He kissed her, pressing her back against the cushions.

"Wait," he said, pulling back. "Let me see your feet."

She raised her legs, showing him her cute pair of snakeskin-patterned flats.

"Very nice. We'll work our way up to spike heels, black stockings, and garter belts by our tenth anniversary."

Mandy chuckled, reaching for him as he swung her legs to the couch and settled in beside her. "I hate to ruin the suspense, but I already have some."

"Don't tell me now. My heart may stop. Just let me love you as you are."

She did, and he lived up to his promise. She smiled, joyous in what they shared, excited by what he did, what she felt free to do to him. Their clothes peeled away, along with her shoes and his boots, until nothing was left but his briefs.

He winced, moving away from her questing hand.

"What's wrong?"

"I have a secret," he said, rolling to his side. He looked a little shy. Much too reserved for Case.

"A secret?"

"A big secret." He rested his hand on the waistband of his white cotton briefs.

Realization dawned. She felt it light up her face. Or was that a blush? She scooted over so she could sit up on the couch.

"Show me."

He looped a hand in the elastic of his briefs and pulled them down.

A perfectly executed, tiny tattoo of a bookworm just like hers, the background a red heart, stared back at her. Her name was even written like text in the book that formed the base of the artwork.

"It's still sore. Someone should have told me not to ride the Harley for two hours after getting tiny needles stuck in my butt."

She fell back, laughing so hard she threatened to dislodge him from the couch. "Oh, Case," she gasped between laughter, "why did you do such a thing? Didn't you know they hurt?"

"I knew." He tentatively rubbed the spot. "Believe me, I'm not into pain." He gazed into her eyes. "But it doesn't hurt as much as losing you."

"You must have been pretty sure of yourself," she said, reaching for his shoulders.

"Very sure. I knew we were kindred spirits when I met you."

"A prissy librarian and a bad-boy biker?"

"Absolutely." He kissed her, pushing her into the

cushions with his weight. Nothing had ever felt better. "A match made in heaven."

"Or in Scotsville," she whispered.

"Doesn't matter," he said between more kisses. "As long as we found each other."

"Case Gardner, you're a hard man to ignore."

"At the moment, Miss Mandy," he said with a sexy drawl, "I'm just a hard man."

He smothered her laughter with kisses, and Mandy knew her heart had found a home.

AUTHOR'S NOTE

I hope you enjoyed this book. If you read my March, 1998, Precious Gem release, *First Love, Last Love,* you know that this story continues in the fictional town of Scottsville, Texas.

On a drive back to Dallas from a writers conference in Shreveport, Louisiana, I thought perhaps I'd driven into *The Twilight Zone* when I saw an exit from I-20 for Scottsville. The town only existed in my book! Later, I learned that it's not on the map, nor does it have a zip code, which explains why I thought it didn't exist! I really did make up the town and inhabitants, but, as usual, fact is stranger than fiction.

I hope you enjoy my books, and I would love to hear from you. Write to Victoria Chancellor, P O Box 852125, Richardson, TX 75085 or e-mail Victoria_Chancellor@compuserve.com. Visit my Web page at www.tlt.com/authors/vchancel.htm for information on my latest releases and previous titles. Thank you, and I hope to hear from you soon.